THE IMMOLATION GAME

MITCHELL TIERNEY

Also By Mitchell Tierney

Young Adult Fiction
Heather Cassidy and the Magnificent Mr Harlow

The Skellington Key

The Wandmaker's Apprentice Series
The Wandmaker's Apprentice

**Everdark Realms Series
with Sabrina RG Raven**
The Darkening
The Awakening

Adult Fiction
Children of the Locomotive

THE IMMOLATION GAME: PHASE ONE

THE IMMOLATION GAME

MITCHELL TIERNEY

The Immolation Game: Phase 01

Published by Ouroborus Book Services
www.ouroborusbooks.com

Cover Design by Sabrina RG Raven
www.sabrinargraven.com

Chapter One: Falling Down

Clank!

The sound of clanging metal echoed around the room. A girl was laying there on a cold, metal bench. She opened her eyes at the noise and was hit with confusion as she wondered where she was and how she got there. The entire ceiling was gleaming with smooth metal panels. She sat up and could hear something rolling around above her. She listened as it moved away, then came back towards her. Whatever it was suddenly dropped, still on the inside of the wall. She swung her feet onto the ground and its chill ran up her legs. Looking down, she noticed the floor was completely made of metal, like the bench, which appeared to be a bed. There was a single blanket and pillow, with nothing else in the room except a pair of white shoes, with white laces. They looked immaculate and new. She slipped them on and gingerly stepped towards the doorway. Outside was a long corridor, and she was the middle door. The doors on her right and left were both closed. Suddenly the door to the right opened. A boy emerged, his eyes wary and slightly confused.

Who is that? she thought to herself. Do I know him?

'Do you hear that?' the boy said.

'It seems to be…' Both of them looked to the right in unison as the clanking noise suddenly changed direction and sounded like it fell again. A whirling noise followed and appeared to come from under them. The boy looked no older than 17. The girl was unsure of her own age. She noticed the hair falling over her face was bleach-blonde and curly. A dull grey staircase leading down was positioned in front of the doors. It looked like it was haphazardly put there. The boy looked back at her, she could see fear and apprehension in his face. He looked utterly terrified.

'What is this place?'

Clang. Clang. Clonk.

There was silence between them as the noise became more distant. The girl sped down the stairs.

'Wait!' the boy yelled.

The girl ignored his pleas and rushed towards the noise. Downstairs was much larger than the level she had just left. There was a lounge room, but instead of couches and tables there were metal blocks, all raised off the ground and made to look like lounges and coffee tables. The noise came closer to her, then passed over her head. Whatever it was, it was moving fast. It seemed to be manoeuvring through some sort of maze or tubing. It hit something, then dropped. It rolled to the left, then the noise moved into another room. The girl followed it. The last room down a long hallway was desolate of any furnishings. It was square and built like a drain. The floor declined into the middle where there was a hole.

'What does this mean?' said a voice behind her. It was the boy. She hadn't heard him come down the stairs. If he was as terrified as he looked, maybe he didn't want to be left alone.

'I don't know, but something is coming this way,' she said.

Four pipes in each corner of the room where the wall met the ceiling all faced the ground. With a loud pop, a metal ball the size of a golf ball spat from the pipe. It hit the ground with an aggressive plonk and started to roll towards the hole.

'Should we stop it?' she asked, unsure if it was a good idea or not.

The boy didn't answer as the ball hit the edge of the hole, bounced up and then slowly dropped into the hole. The whole house started to rumble and shake.

'Is it an earthquake?' the boy asked, moving quickly into a crouched position.

'Get outside!' the girl screamed, running toward the front door. There was an open frame, with no door on it.

'Help!' came a scream from upstairs as they reached the front porch.

The boy turned around, 'Someone else is here?'

The girl ran back into the foyer and up the stairs.

'Wait!' he yelled, 'Don't go back in there! This whole place is going to fall down.'

The girl ignored him. She ran up to the second floor and down the hallway. There was a young girl by the third bedroom with short rose-red hair trying to keep balanced by holding onto the doorframe.

'This way!'

The red-headed girl was hesitant, but her hesitation gave way to trust and she followed her down the stairs and outside.

Chapter Two: Go By

The grass outside felt tough when they walked on it. It had the same texture as plastic. But that thought was fleeting as they noticed above them, the sky was metal and in the distance were metal walls. They were in a large metal room. The boy looked up at the two-story structure they had just run from. It looked like a house on the inside and from the outside, but there was something different about it. The walls seemed thicker. It had been vibrating and shaking violently, but it suddenly stopped.

'Where are we?' the girl said.

The boy looked confused as he gazed around the lawn in front of them. There was a large, stainless-steel wall encircling the house. The few trees there all looked crooked and welded from metal. Their branches appeared sharp and still.

'Look,' said the red-head girl. She was pointing towards the wall. A small hole, about chest height was staring at them like an inky black eye.

The girl stepped up to it and tried to look inside. 'What is it for?' she asked, knowing no one would know the answer.

The boy ran his fingers along a square hatch that was built into the wall just left of the hole. He tried to slide his fingers into the niche, but it was too small. He pushed on every corner, but nothing would budge.

'I have no idea,' he replied. His face dropped as he looked around to the girls again, then at his own hands. They seemed foreign to him, like he was seeing them for the first time.

'Do you… remember anything?'

'It feels like a dream,' the girl with the blonde hair said.

The boy ran his long fingers through his soft, brown hair.

'This is too much.' He instinctively placed his hands into the pockets of his white pants, which he hadn't had time to notice they were all wearing. Something was at the bottom of one of the deep pockets. He pulled a small, rectangular piece of paper out and stared at it.

'What's that?' the blonde girl said. She looked the same age as the boy, and they were nearly equal in height.

He unfolded the small parchment. 'Ranunculus,' he said quizzically, his eyebrows knotting together in confusion.

The red headed girl checked her pockets, finding her own slip of paper, 'Nerium?'

Finally, the girl with blonde hair slid her hand into her pocket and pulled out her folded piece of paper, 'Delphinium.'

'What does it mean?'

'Maybe it's a clue? Something we say?'

'They're our names,' Delphinium said, looking around at the ceiling far above them.

'Ranunculus?' the boy said, slipping the paper back into his pocket. 'I would say, if it is my name, I would have gone by Rann, or Cul.'

'Which do you think you would have preferred?' Nerium said.

'Guys, look,' Delphinium said, stepping away from the hole in the wall. The corner of a wire cage could be seen towards the east side of the house. She took a few more steps to see what it was. A large aviary had been constructed on the fake grass.

Nerium and Rann both followed Delphinium as she gingerly walked around the odd metallic house to the large cage made of wire and steel. It was five meters high and just as wide. Nerium placed her fingers in the wire and pushed her face against it.

'No birds?'

'Why have an aviary and no birds?' Rann added.

Delphinium ran her fingers around the edge of the cage until she reached the door. There was no lock on it, only a sliding mechanism. She slid it across, and the door opened on its own. She looked up to see a dull metal ceiling. Filling the aviary were metal trees with hundreds of branches and twigs. Rann and Nerium stayed outside.

'I wouldn't go in there,' said Rann.

'There's no sign that it had ever been used for any animals.'

'Don't you think it's weird we can remember what birds are, but not our own names?'

Delphinium turned to Rann. He was right, but there was something more pressing on her thoughts. It was as if something was trying to come into her mind but was covered in a fog. She tried to reach further into her brain, way back to her childhood, but it was blurry. Then, from inside the house came a distant noise.

Clank!

'Did you hear that?'

'It's the same noise as before,' Rann said, moving away from the aviary and towards the house.

Delphinium stepped out of the cage and listened. It was coming from inside the house. She ran towards the back door, grabbing the handle, but it wouldn't budge.

'It's stuck,' she gasped.

'Look,' Rann said, pointing to the bottom of the door. It was welded to the frame.

Delphinium stepped back and looked up at the second level. She could hear the ball sliding around mechanisms and hitting latches that pushed it in other directions. She ran around the house and in through the front doorway. Nerium and Rann followed her in.

'It's upstairs!' Nerium said, running up the stairs, her red hair streaming behind her.

'Wait,' Rann yelped. 'It's coming down here.'

Delphinium looked towards the room she had seen earlier with the hole in the ground. 'In here,' she said and sprinted into the vacant room. She looked up, tracing the ball as it came closer.

'Should we actually be stopping it?' Nerium asked, staring up at the ceiling.

'If you want to find answers… we have to do something,' Delphinium replied as the ball slid down the wall and spat out of the exposed pipe. Delphinium leapt towards it, her hands outstretched. The ball was polished metal and slipped straight through her hands, hitting the floor with a loud clang. Rann bolted forward, diving onto the ground. His long arms snatched the ball seconds before it disappeared down the hole.

'You got it!' Nerium hollered joyously. Her smile was from ear to ear.

Rann stood up, looking at the ball. 'It's just… a ball?'

'Maybe it's meant to go down the hole?'

Rann offered the ball to Delphinium, 'The hole in the wall outside?'

Nerium looked from Delphinium to Rann. 'What if… it releases something?'

'Only one way to find out,' Rann said excited, snatching the ball from Delphinium.

'Rann, wait!' Delphinium said, running after him.

Rann bolted outside and reached the hole in the wall, just as Delphinium caught up to him.

'Shouldn't we think this through first?'

Rann grinned, 'It went down the other hole Delphi, and nothing happened…maybe this is a way out.'

'No. Something did happen… it made the house shake!'

He pinched the ball between his index finger and thumb and pushed it into the hole without regard for what Delphi had said. A loud ringing alarm sounded. Nerium had followed them, covering her ears until she was in visual range of the hole. She then squeezed her eyes shut tight in case something came out of the chute. The outline of the square within the wall opened with a violent burst.

Delphi reluctantly peered inside.

Chapter Three: The Answer

'What's in it?' Rann asked, slightly regretting being so hasty in his actions.

Delphi stared at the contents. It was a chute with a metal bottom. Folded up were three extra blankets and a fire-starting kit with flint and steel in a plastic bag. Delphi reached in and started handing them to Rann.

'How are we going to start a fire if everything here is metal?' Rann quizzed.

Nerium took one of the blankets and draped it over her shoulders.

'Maybe they want us to burn these?'

Delphi looked at the fire starter. She had a strange feeling in her gut. It was as if this place was giving them an indication of things to come.

That night, the two girls sat in Nerium's room and spoke. Rann was outside checking the aviary and the surroundings for anything he could make a fire with.

'What do you think this is?' Nerium said, her face clearly distressed. Her eyes had turned red and she had been biting her nails. She pulled the blanket off and rewrapped it around her body.

'I'm not sure. It feels like a dream. I know basic things like the sky and trees and fire, but I can't remember who I am. What was my name before? Who are my parents? What did I do? Did I grow up here?'

Nerium choked back tears. 'Do you think we are in some sort of prison?'

The air inside was starting to get cooler. Delphi pulled the other blanket over her shoulders and wrapped it around her neck like a scarf.

'There must be a way out… and an answer, we just need to find it.'

'An answer to what? Why we are here? Like this is some kind of puzzle?'

'I guess so.'

'What if it's not? What if it's the end of the world, and we're the only survivors?' Nerium said, her voice shaking.

'Someone is running the machines that opens the chutes, right?' Delphi replied. 'Someone is releasing the balls… there's got to be others out there.' There was silence for several seconds before Delphi spoke again. 'If they're giving us things we need, then it has to be a game.'

'They aren't giving us food and I'm starving,' Nerium said, standing up. She had become frustrated with the endless questions and no answers.

'Where are you going?'

'See if Rann found anything.'

Rann was by the aviary looking at all the metal trees. He traced his finger along a welding mark at the base. It was done with precision, by someone who had experience. He didn't know how he knew it, but he did. He stood up and continued investigating the other trees, trying to find something that would give him a clue to what was going on. There were trees scattered outside the aviary as well. They were all taller, with thicker trunks and razor sharp, metal leaves. He leapt up and grasped one of the branches, pulling himself up. He continued climbing upwards until he was high enough to see over the room. He sat on a branch and looked out past the walled off area. Everything was covered in dull, flat metal sheets. He reached up and wrapped his arms around the next branch, pulling himself up higher than the house. Looking up, he could see he was halfway to the ceiling.

'I wouldn't go any higher,' Nerium said, from several metres below.

'I think I can see something up here,' Rann mumbled back. The metal sky above them appeared to go on forever, but once Rann got closer, he could see more details of the construction. There were several lights along the fake sky. They were flat against the panels, replicating the same illumination as sunlight. 'I might be able to unscrew it and slip through,' he said, squinting his eyes.

'Rann, I wouldn't.'

Rann pushed upwards, and then his foot was suddenly slipping on the dull metal beam that was in the shape of a branch. He fell backwards, slamming hard against another branch behind him, falling towards the ground.

'Rann!' Nerium screamed running towards him.

Inside the house, Delphi heard the gut-churning howl and sprinted outside. She could see Rann on the ground with Nerium screaming. She was standing over him. Rann had fallen and hit several metal branches before hitting the ground and crumbling into an unconscious heap. Delphi bolted past Nerium and slid on her knees to Rann.

'Rann! Can you hear me?' She rolled him over onto his back. His nose was bleeding. She moved her hands over his arms and legs, nothing felt broken. 'Rann... Rann,' she kept repeating.

Nerium approached gingerly, tears streaming down her face. 'Rann?'

His eyes gently opened and closed again.

'Is it your back?' Delphi asked, peeling his eyelids back. His eyes rolled down and looked at her.

'I'm... okay,' he said. His words were laboured. 'My arm hurts so badly. I think it's broken.'

'It might be fractured... we need to get you inside onto your bed.'

Nerium wrapped Rann's good arm over her shoulders and helped Delphi lift him up. He moaned when he got to his feet, refusing to put weight on them.

'My foot... it's swollen... hurts so bad.'

Delphi was careful with his injured arm, taking him inside and laying him on the bed in his room. He laid on his back as Nerium fetched another blanket. She rolled it up and placed it under his swollen foot.

'There is nothing to eat here. We need food… and water,' Nerium said, looking towards Delphi.

'We need to wait for the next ball… hopefully it will give us something else we need,' she said desperately.

Nerium went to her room and laid down, her mind was racing. She cried until she fell asleep.

Delphi sat with Rann until he was asleep. It took what seemed like hours, but she couldn't be sure. Time was strange and artificial here, just like the grass and sky. She couldn't tell if she was asleep for 5 minutes or an hour. Slowly, with her eyes drooping, she moved to her bedroom and laid on her bed. She tried to let her mind wander free, trying to secure a memory or image of her past life, but something kept it from floating from thought to thought. Every time something was about to appear, a white dull light took it away. She shook her head and tried to clear the light. Soon she realised she must have dozed off because when she woke, the temperature had dropped dramatically. She could now see her breath as she exhaled. She pulled the blanket up under her chin and tried to stay awake, listening for the next ball.

Clank!

Delphi sat bolt upright, above her she could hear the ball sliding down from the roof and into the ceiling. It ran across the wall that separated her room from Rann's. She leapt to her feet and ran downstairs, ignoring where it went. Latches clinked and mechanisms pushed it around the house as she entered the drain room. She stood over the hole, blocking it with her foot. The ball popped out of the exit pipe behind her, bounced across the floor and rolled to a full stop at her foot. She bent down and picked it up as Nerium appeared, blurry eyed.

'You got one!' she said elated.

Delphi didn't spend any time studying the ball in her hand, she ran outside and stumbled in shock as a hooded figure stood in the darkness. She opened her mouth to scream, but nothing came out. The figure turned quickly. It wore a hazmat suit. Its face was hidden in a mask and it was draped in black cloth. Nerium came out behind Delphi and yelped, covering her mouth in fear. The figure slammed the delivery chute closed and took off running towards an open door, where another figure stood. Delphi dropped the ball and ran towards them. She pushed her fear aside in order to get answers.

'Delphi!' Nerium yelled, reaching out to stop her.

'Who are you?!'

The figures disappeared into the door and slammed it shut behind them.

Chapter Four: Life Before this One

Delphi picked the ball back up and handed it to Nerium.

'How long were we asleep for?' Nerium asked, holding the ball up to the hole.

'It's still dark. I have no idea. Seemed like a few hours.'

She pushed the ball into the hole. It slid down its metal ramp and rattled before finally *clank*ing and being swallowed by cogs and chain driven drives. The chute popped open. Delphi rushed to it, holding it open.

'What is it?'

'Looks like a jug of water and a loaf of bread!' Delphi said excitedly.

The chute started to close. Delphi snatched everything out of it, placing it on the floor. She spun around, gripping the edges of the chute, trying to hold it open. She could see into the darkness at the far end. The chute screeched as its cog-teeth jammed along its chains. It was far too strong for her and slammed shut, narrowly missing her fingers. Nerium picked up the jug, it was unlike anything she had ever seen, or thought she had ever seen. It looked like it only held several litres, but it was much heavier. On top of the lid was a filtration system. Delphi picked up the loaf of bread, now slightly dinted in one corner. It still felt soft and warm.

'Is this some form of torture?' Nerium said, walking with Delphi back inside. 'Did I do something in a previous life that got me here?'

Delphi placed the bread on the kitchen counter and tried one of the cupboards. The first two were empty, but the third held three metal cups. The thinness of the cups made them nearly see-through. She poured some water into a cup and tore off a piece of bread.

'I'll take this up to Rann, you start eating.' She went up the staircase and along the hallway to his room. Rann stirred from his slumber and sat up.

'Oh, hey,' he said. 'What's all the commotion? Was there another ball?' Delphi almost dropped the cup. Her eyes were wide open. 'What is it?' Rann looked down. Rann's leg was wrapped in a brace, as was his arm. Leaning on the wall to his right were crutches, made of metal, except for the ends, which were padded.

'What…' Rann said, sitting up and swinging his leg off the bed. 'Who did this?' His voice was shaking.

'We…' Delphi gathered her nerves. 'We got another ball and it gave us food and water.'

'This isn't right,' Rann started to panic. 'This is too weird.' Rann had reached the end of his tether. 'Who is doing this to us? If I could just talk to them, maybe they would let us go? Maybe this is a mistake… we aren't meant to be here.'

Delphi placed the bread and water on the side table and went to him. She gently held his hands. They felt rough, with strange callouses.

'Listen, we will get through this… I promise. Whatever is happening, and whoever they are, they are playing with us. They want us to break.'

'How do you know?' His eyes were watery with tears.

'I don't, but we need to remain calm and keep a level head…understood?' Rann nodded. 'If you want to, come downstairs and eat with us. We can help you down the stairs.'

She wanted to tell him about the masked figures she saw and the door, but he was in no mental state to hear it, yet. Rann reached for the crutches and hobbled over to the staircase. Delphi helped him down while Nerium went up to his room and brought down his bread and water.

'Do you think,' Rann started, 'we knew each other in our other life? The life before this one?'

'I don't know if I could have been friends with someone called Ranunculus,' Delphi joked.

Nerium laughed while Rann stifled a smile. 'Very funny,' he said.

Nerium began, 'Do you think if each ball gives us something different… soon we will have a way out?'

Delphi didn't like predicting what would happen in this place. Everything was far too random. She wanted to tell them it would be okay, but deep in her mind she wasn't sure herself.

'Could be,' Rann said, with a mouth full of bread. 'Maybe if we give it two balls, they'll give us pizza.'

'Pizza?' Nerium replied, a big smile on her face. 'I remember pizza… I know I like it, but it's hard to think of what it tasted like.' She jokingly hit the side of her head with the palm of her hand.

Delphi was staring at the metal crutches that Rann had leant against the bench.

'What are you thinking?' Rann said, tracing her eyesight. 'Do you want to take them for a spin?'

'I'm thinking… it's a crazy idea, but…'

Nerium stood up, 'Tell us.'

'One of those crutches could be strong enough to….'

'You want to throw one down there?'

'No,' Delphi replied, 'I want to jam it open.'

Rann looked at the crutch quizzically. 'It might work.'

'Problem is,' Delphi added, 'the chute isn't very big, we couldn't wedge it open, we would have to use our strength and hold it open. I've seen down the chute… it's not very big. We would need someone small enough.'

Rann looked at Nerium. 'You could fit.'

'Hey!' Nerium said, stepping back from the counter. 'I'm not going in the chute, who knows what's down there.'

'It's gotta be a delivery area, right?' Delphi said. 'Like a place they can place the food and blankets they've given us. It shouldn't be anything dangerous.'

'But what if it is?' Nerium said.

'What if we jam it open and you climb in and look… then come back straight away?' Rann said, pouring water into his cup.

'What if the crutch snaps and closes on my leg?'

'I've felt the pressure... it's strong, but not that strong.'

Nerium felt a kinship to Rann and Delphi, but that didn't stop her from feeling nervous.

'Okay,' she said, placing a piece of bread in her mouth and finding she didn't have the motivation to chew it. Her mind was already humming with trepidation.

'We'll wait for the next ball and try it.'

During the night, Rann got up. He was restless and in pain. He hobbled around the yard near the aviary to try to get some fresh air, if that was possible through the false ceiling. He studied the trees and tried to work out how they had been built. He ran his fingers along the trunks, noting their shape and how they had been crafted with a small hammer. The indents were small and round. Nerium sat on the porch and stared at the chute. She was biting her nails and kept talking to herself. She was discussing how she would do it. How she would get her head down the chute and look. Her stomach was in knots. Delphi had gone to the drain room and sat right near the hole. She had noticed there was a slight breeze coming out of the hole. She crawled over to it on her hands and knees and looked down into the darkness. She could hear the whirling of engines and the soft drone of conveyor belts. From far above her came the now familiar *clank*! She leapt to her feet and looked upwards as Rann and Nerium come around the side of the house. Nerium was running, surprised at the noise from the falling ball. Rann was out of breath from trying to keep up. They finally got to the room as the ball slid back and forth through the house.

'You heard that?' Rann said, rocking from side to side on his crutches.

'Yeah, it's coming,' Delphi replied, keeping her eyes focused on the ceiling above her.

The sound came from deep within the house. It rattled and popped as it changed tracks, then stopped suddenly and was pushed back the other way. Nerium walked out of the room.

'It's going in a different direction than the others,' she

speculated.

Then the noise appeared near the stairs, as if it were in the railings. Suddenly, it shot out of the pipe facing Delphi. She wasn't going to miss it this time. Swinging her hand towards it, she nabbed it out of the air so quick Rann nearly missed it.

'I think you may have played some sport in your old life,' Rann said, impressed.

'I don't miss twice,' she added.

They gathered outside. Nerium knew the time had come. She had spent the last hour or two getting herself physically and mentally ready. Nerium was the first to reach the chute. Delphi looked at her. She was worried also.

'You don't have to do this,' she said, in a tone that resembled a big sister giving a little sister a stern warning.

'I can do it. It may be our only way out.'

'If something goes wrong,' Delphi said, her voice sounding a little strained, 'we will get you out.'

Rann placed one crutch on the wall and held the other. Nerium got herself ready in front of the hatch. Delphi held the ball at the entrance of the hole. She nodded to everyone to see if they were ready. They nodded back. She let the ball slide in. The hollow gulping sound faded quickly as something deep below them turned and rotated. The chute spat open. Rann lifted his crutch and jammed it between the wall and the mouth of the latch. It just fit. He then gripped it with all his might, making his muscles bulge through his shirt. Delphi rushed over and held it open, her knuckles turning white. Nerium looked inside, there was a bag tied with a red ribbon. She snatched it and tossed it to the ground, then clambered in. She could feel hot hair coming through small nooks toward the rear of the chute. It smelt of oil and grease. Through a slight separation in the metal, Nerium could see someone moving. Suddenly, the chute slammed shut, knocking Delphi onto her back. Rann almost had his fingers caught. Whatever had ordered the latch close, it did it with malevolent intent.

'Did she make it?' Rann said, hobbling as he noticed the hatch closed with Nerium and his crutch inside it.

'She did,' Delphi said, getting to her feet and running to the outline of the chute. 'Nerium!' she called out. 'Can you hear me? Are you okay?'

There was no response. The lights above them flicked, then went out.

Chapter Five: Butchers Paper

'Delphi?' Rann said, lifting his bad leg off the ground to take the weight off it.

'I'm here,' Delphi responded. 'Whoever is in charge didn't like what we just did.'

'Did you see anything before the lights went out?'

'I couldn't see a damn thing,' Rann said, frustrated.

The air around them was becoming increasingly cooler.

Delphi felt around the wall for the outline of the chute. After finding it, she tried to pry it open. It hadn't worked before, but she had to try. She felt guilty for encouraging Nerium to go inside the chute.

'Nerium!' she hollered. She banged her fist on the wall. A slight echo could be heard through the metal.

'She's gone,' Rann said, putting his hand on her shoulder. 'Whoever is on the other side has her now. Maybe she's free?'

'The thing is,' Delphi said, stepping back, 'we don't know.'

'Grab the bag, we better go inside,' Rann said, moving his hand around until he found his one remaining crutch. There were no lights on inside the house. They moved along the walls, feeling their way to the kitchen. They had a vague outline in their heads of the floorplan, but not enough to orientate without assistance. Rann felt for the metal chair and sat down, waiting for his eyes to adjust. He could hear Delphi's breathing. She sounded like she was hyperventilating.

'Delph?'

'I'm here.'

'What's in the bag?'

'It feels like… wood? And paper.'

'For a fire?'

'I'm not sure. It would make sense since they gave us the flint.'

A dull blue light illuminated outside, spilling a cobalt wave of rippled light across the kitchen floor. Rann and Delphi both turned their heads towards the open front door.

'Stay here,' Delphi said.

'Don't go out there,' Rann pleaded, reaching for his crutch to get back on his feet.

'I'm just going to look.'

Delphi paced slowly until she reached the doorway. The lights in the ceiling were now blue. It gave off just enough light to see the floor.

'What do you see?' Rann shouted, straining his neck to see her.

Suddenly, from micro spouts in the walls came the sound of hissing.

'Can you hear that?' Delphi said, and instantly started to feel disorientated.

'Delphi!' Rann said, before collapsing backwards.

Delphi ran towards him, but she only got a few steps before tumbling to her knees and falling unconscious on the floor.

Clank!

Delphi opened her eyes and she was staring at the ceiling again. Her stomach felt queasy and her lungs hurt. She leapt to her feet and ran out of her room and down the stairs. With each hammering footstep, her joints ached.

The ball dropped down to the ground level and bounced through the west wall, then spat out of the pipe. Delphi reached the drain room and threw herself at the ground, only to watch the ball roll down into the hole and disappear. She laid there and watched her breath plume out of her mouth.

'So close,' came an unfamiliar voice from behind her.

Delphi looked towards the door and saw a woman standing there, looking confused. She had long brown hair, dead-straight, with plump lips and delicate long fingers. She looked several years older than Delphi and Rann. Delphi stood up, very apprehensive. She took a gentle step back and readied her hands by her side.

'Who are you?'

The woman thought for a moment, 'I don't know. Is it me, or is it freezing cold in here?'

'Did you come from upstairs?'

'I woke up in one of the rooms. I saw you running down here.'

From behind her Rann appeared. His thoughts were still with Nerium.

'This is messed up,' Rann said aggressively. 'They are drugging us then putting us in the beds?'

The woman turned around, and only then did Rann realise someone else was in the house.

'Wait, who are you?'

'I don't know,' she responded, turning back to Delphi. 'What is this place? How did I get here?' She looked at Rann and Delphi. They were dressed the same as her and looked equally confused.

'We woke up here too. We had the same reaction when we woke up. We are friendly,' Delphi said, forcing a smile even though she was still upset with Nerium having disappeared.

'Check your pockets,' Rann said, hobbling past her.

The woman slipped her hands into her pockets. With her left hand, she pulled out a small piece of paper.

'Clematis?' she read aloud.

'I'm Ranunculus and that's Delphinium.'

'Poisonous flowers,' Clematis said.

'What? What did you say?' Delphi said, walking towards her.

'They are names of poisonous flowers.'

Rann looked at Delphi, his mouth agape.

'Why would they give us poisonous flower names?' Rann said, mostly to himself while he was deep in thought.

'I go by Delphi, and we call him Rann, makes things easier,' Delphi said as they followed her into the kitchen where the bag from the chute was sitting on a bench.

'I'll be Clem. So, do you know a way out?'

'Not that we can tell,' Rann said, opening the bag and pulling out its contents.

Long pieces of wood, followed by small twigs and sticks, then butchers' paper and soft newspaper without anything printed on it.

'I think I know a way out,' Delphi said, now feeling slightly guilty for keeping this information from Rann.

Rann looked at her, 'You do?'

'We saw cloaked figures run back in through a door. They were wearing hazmat suits, with helmets. Big helmets, with screens down over their faces. They had on these drapes, like long coats. It was all in black.'

'When were you going to tell me this?' Rann said.

Clem sat on the bench. Normally anyone would feel awkward, but Clem ingested the conversation, as if she thrived on the drama.

'I meant to, Rann. It's just, with the loss the Nerium… then…' Delphi trailed off, knowing she had made a mistake.

'Guys,' Clem said. 'Fighting is the last thing we need. We have to get out of here, right?'

Rann nodded as he started assembling the firewood into a pile to carry. He left the room and went down the hall to one of the bedrooms. Delphi followed, wanting to apologise. This room was bigger. It had a window to the aviary, but it wasn't glass that filled the frame, it was Perspex. The room had several long, metal benches pressed against the far wall. On the east wall was an odd-looking fireplace. It had no mantle, just an egg-shaped hole from the ground, going up several feet. Rann stuck his head inside it and looked up.

'Yup, as I guessed, a fireplace.'

'How did you know it was in here? I hadn't seen it before.' Delphi said.

'I guess we both need to work on our secret keeping, right?'

Rann stacked the fireplace. He knew where the wood should go, and he placed the paper through the bottom of it.

The wood tilted up to a summit. He stood up and marvelled at his creation. He knew he had done it before, several times. It came natural to him. He turned and headed out of the room.

'Where are you going?' Clem asked, standing in the hallway. She had followed them but stopped short of the doorway.

'To get the fire starter.'

'Should we wait till night?' Delphi said.

Rann took several steps back into the room. He was walking without his crutch now, but his leg still hurt. The swelling had gone down since he had been knocked out by the gas.

'When's night, Delphi? When's day? When are we being fed in this lunatic asylum? How do we know what is what?' his voice quivered with frustration. He sat down, knowing perfectly well he had lost his temper. 'Look, I'm sorry. It's just getting too much for me.'

Clem sat beside him. 'Let's go through what we know and work our way up from there? Yeah?'

'A metal ball is released at random intervals,' Delphi said, staring at the unlit wood temple.

'You feed it into this hole in the wall… and it gives you what you need. The first time, we got blankets, pillows and the fire-starting kit.'

'The second time it was bread and water.'

'Then what?' Clem asked.

'We jammed the hatch open and Nerium went inside.'

Delphi caught herself before bursting into tears. The lump in her throat made it hard to swallow, but she pushed it down, trying to stay strong.

Clem looked from Rann to Delphi. 'There was another person here before me?'

Rann nodded sadly, also feeling somewhat at fault for agreeing with the plan for her to go inside the latch. But he continued, 'There's an aviary outside. All the trees are made of metal.'

'How did you hurt your leg?'

'I climbed a tree, all the way up to the ceiling to look at the light fixtures,' Rann went over to the wood pile and picked up a stick, looked at it and put it back. He picked up another and stared at the end.

'Why?'

'I wanted to see if there was a way out. Maybe unscrew the lights and get into the ceiling.'

He slipped the length of wood into his pocket.

'The house shook, I remember,' Delphi said, her mind suddenly jolting.

'Shook?'

'When we missed one of the balls. The first one, I think. The whole house shook like an earthquake.'

'When I woke up here, I walked out of the room and down the stairs. I saw you run into that other room,' Clem said, pointing in the direction of the room. 'I saw the ball go down the hole, but there was no earthquake.'

Delphi nodded, 'That one went down quicker. It didn't follow the same path through the house that the others did. Maybe that has something to do with it?'

'But what I mean is... you missed a ball and something bad happened. Now we've missed another one.'

Delphi looked at Rann.

'The house didn't shake this time,' Rann said, standing near the Perspex window.

'But something bad should happen, right?' Clem said.

Delphi looked at her. 'Then we need to prepare if something bad is about to happen.'

Chapter Six: Nowhere to Go

Tap, tap, tap.

Delphi opened her eyes. She was staring at the ceiling again. The sound was soft and constant. She sat up, remembering she put herself to bed after watching Rann light the fire and sitting with everyone around it to keep warm. They had all tried to remember their past, but memories were blurry and full of grey static.

From above, the tapping became more incessant. It wasn't in a distinct pattern or structure, it was random. She walked out of her room and looked in the next one. She could see Clem lying on her stomach, her back moving up and down, gently sleeping. She went to the next room and saw Rann. He was snoring, with one leg off the bed and his blanket wrapped around his waist. She went downstairs as the tapping continued. It became more frequent and heavier as she put distance between herself and the rooms.

Inside the lounge, where the fireplace was, she looked at the ashes. There were no embers, or smoke. It had long gone out. Something jogged her memory. A camping trip perhaps. Something distant in her mind showed itself, then was quickly taken away. Rain? She thought. That sound. Something about camping in the rain. She went to the door and looked outside. It had started to rain. It came down heavy from the ceiling far above. She squinted her eyes but could only see a misty rain cloud overhead. Micro-sprinklers were spraying water all over the house and surroundings. Drops slipped off the polished metal railing that ran the length of the porch and pooled in front of the steps with nowhere to go.

'What's going on?' Clem said behind her. She was still half

asleep. Moving her hair from her face, she yawned and stretched. 'It's difficult sleeping on that hard, metal bed.'

'It's raining.'

'But… how?'

Delphi pointed to the far corner of the roof. Several of the sprinklers could be seen through the haze.

'We should fill our jug up. It should be drinkable.'

Clem went inside to fetch the jug. When she returned, she walked straight out into the rain. Delphi smiled and wanted to join her, but it was too cold. The environment turned increasingly cooler with each passing hour. It was now at the point of being freezing. Clem danced in the rain with great self-confidence. She flailed her hands around and placed the jug in the centre of the front yard.

'You should come out Delphi!' she said, grinning widely. 'It's magnificent!'

The rain poured down on her, soaking her white pants and shirt. She was barefoot and danced like she was on her own, in her bedroom, with music playing. Suddenly, she stopped dead still… Her smile quickly faded. Clem's arms went to her side and she stepped back very slowly, her eyes peeled open, looking forward.

'What's wrong?' Delphi said. 'Did it get too cold?'

'Delph,' Clem said, nearly at a whisper.

Delphi tried to see what she was staring at, but whatever it was, was in the dark mist of the yard.

'What's wrong?'

'Run!' she screamed and bolted back to the house.

Delphi stood, frozen to the spot as Clem bolted passed her. From the foggy mist came a creature walking on all fours. It was massive. Hunched over and walking as if it was savouring the stalking of its prey. Its elongated snout and long ears were characteristics that Delphi suddenly recognised. A wolf, her brain told her. Its long grey fur was dripping wet and its lips were peeled back, exposing long, pearl-white fangs. Deep within its sockets were yellow eyes peering out of narrow slitted eyelids. Delphi stepped backwards through the doorway without taking her eyes off it.

'Rann,' she said. 'Rann!'

She turned and sped up the staircase to Rann's room, he was already at the doorway. He heard the terror in her voice.

'What is it? What's wrong?'

'There's something outside,' she gasped, looking over the banister of the second level.

The ginormous wolf slowly paced inside and stopped. Rann audibly gasped. The creature's breathing could be heard like a war drum, carrying through the house.

'What the hell,' Rann finally said, his voice shaking. 'Where's Clem?'

The wolf suddenly snapped to attention and took a step back as Clem came into view. She held a long length of half burnt wood. The end was on fire.

'Get back!' she screamed at the huge beast. 'Back!'

The wolf growled, exposing more of its rear teeth. Its red tongue darted out of its mouth. Clem stepped forward, jabbing the stick towards the wolf until it was outside. There was no door to shut, so she slowly, without taking her eyes of the animal, placed the fire stick on the ground, right in the middle of the doorway.

'Clem!' Delphi yelped, running to the stairs.

'What the hell is that thing doing in here!' Rann hollered, hobbling away from the staircase.

Clem made her way up the stairs by walking backwards. She was too afraid to take her eyes off the doorway. The wolf had now disappeared into the foggy cloud in the yard.

'How did you know it would hate fire?' Rann asked, looking at her, his eyes still popeyed.

'Most animals would run from fire.'

Rann felt his heart slow in his chest.

'That fire won't burn for much longer.'

'Is it the only way in and out?' Clem asked.

'Yeah,' Rann answered. 'There's a window in the kitchen, too small for that thing to fit through and a window in the fire-place room.'

'That thing's going to get hungrier, if it's not starving already,' Delphi said, looking from Clem to the small flame in the doorway. It was burning through the wood quickly.

'What do we do?' Rann asked, the same quiver still in his voice.

Clem looked to Delphi, 'We kill it.'

'We don't have anything to kill it with.'

'The ball,' Delph said. 'Maybe the house will provide us with something we need. It has so far.'

'It just means one of us has to go out there… to the hole in the wall.'

All three looked through the doorway into the rain as the yard continued to fill with water.

Chapter Seven: The Hunt

Rann took his brace off and laid it on the floor of his room. He bent his leg and lifted it up. It felt fine, but he still wasn't sure if he could run on it. They had decided to take turns keeping watch at the front door. Beside Delphi was a pile of wood, ready to burn. A small bundle of hot ash and the fire starter. Delphi knelt down and tried to look through the flowing mist but could only see grey clouds and shadows. Clem was up in her bedroom doorway, leaning on the frame.

'You know, if we each have fire, we could all huddle together and make it to the hole.'

'What's to say that thing won't just attack us all? It's bigger than two of us combined… you saw its teeth.'

'Well,' Clem said, looking around the corner at Rann. 'What's your bright idea? We can't keep it outside forever.'

'We trap it.'

Clem stopped leaning and lent over the balcony to see Delphi by the front door. 'Where?'

'In the aviary. It has a door and a latch on the outside.'

'How are we going to get it in there?'

'We'll bait it. There's a small amount of bread left.'

'Wolves don't eat bread. They're carnivores.'

'Do you have a better idea?'

Clem looked at him. 'I'll entice it in.'

'You?'

'Do you want to do it, with your leg?'

'How are you going to entice it in?'

'I'll lure it in by being in there.'

'There's no way.'

From the front door Delphi yelled out, 'What? There is no way you're luring it into the cage by actually being in it.'

Clem looked down to her feet, then over the ledge to Delphi. 'Once it's in there with me, I'll start a fire and move my way around the cage till I reach the door, then you will let me out and we'll lock it.'

'And the wolf?'

'It dies.'

Rann walked to the staircase without his brace or crutch. Delphi looked up at him.

'We get the fire ready, from the outside… as soon as it enters, we start the fire and pass it to you.'

Clem looked at Rann. 'Okay.'

'I still don't like this idea,' Rann said nervously.

'It's either that, or one of us falls asleep on watch and we all die.'

'Surely they can't keep it in here forever?'

'Well, how long are we going to be kept in here for, Rann?'

Rann turned his back to Clem. He wanted to yell, or to go out there himself and try and take down the wolf alone. Part of him felt completely exhausted from his injury and the strangeness of this place, the other part wanted it to end, somehow.

'Okay,' he finally said. 'I'll get more wood.'

They met by the door where Delphi was waiting with the fire she had started and a handful of long pieces of wood. Rann still looked nervous. He held his crutch out like a shield, testing out its manoeuvrability. Clem came down the stairs with a hard expression.

'Ready?'

Rann and Delphi both nodded. Together they all walked outside and down the stairs to the front yard. The air was chilly and moved around the house like a slow moving whirlwind. Delphi shivered in her thin clothes. She regretted not wrapping the blanket around her.

'Can you see it?' Rann said. All three had their backs to one another.

'No.'

'I can't even hear it.'

'Maybe they took it away?'

The lights were dimmed to the point of putting them in nearly complete darkness. The mist floated along the cold metal flooring, covering the surroundings in a coat of heavy, grey fog. Rann started a flame on the end of his stick by holding it to Delphi's lit torch. He held it up in front of him.

'This way,' Rann said, leading the way to the aviary.

The darkness swallowed them eagerly. Fog licked at their feet as the inky night gave way to the short, flickering flame. Rann felt Delphi grip his arm. She held the wooden stick out in front of her like a spear. Clem was so close they stepped on each other's shoes.

'This house is way bigger on the outside, you notice that?'

Rann was too busy looking out for the wolf to notice. Delphi glanced to the side and saw a large shadow following them.

'It's here,' she announced at a whisper.

Rann stopped suddenly. 'Where?'

'Keep walking,' Clem ordered. 'It's hunting us.'

Rann hated the sound of that. Being watched by something he couldn't see gave him gooseflesh on his neck and arms. The flame's light started to reveal the wire fence a few yards in front of them. Clem stopped abruptly.

Delphi could sense how fearful Clem was. 'You don't have to do this, Clem. We'll figure something out.'

From behind them they heard the pounding of feet sprinting towards them.

'There's no time,' Clem yelled. 'Everyone get in the cage!'

Chapter Eight: Bait

In her panic, Delphi tried to slam the door shut behind them, but the wolf pushed its way in, knocking the torch out of her hand with the force. Rann also dropped his firestick in fear and it hit the ground, extinguishing instantly. They were in total darkness. There was a loud howl, then thumping across the metal ground. Rann screamed and was knocked down. Delphi couldn't see anything except the small glows of the embers which were casting shadows across the ground.

'Rann!' she screamed.

'Delphi, get back,' Clem ordered. Delphi could hear Clem's voice from the ground to her left.

Bright yellow sparks lit the small enclosure. Delphi looked to where they were coming from and could see Clem on the ground, trying to start a small fire. She had paper and the remaining tinder in front of her. Her eyes were focused forward, instead of down. Delphi looked up and could see the giant wolf hunched over Rann. There was already blood on the ground. Delphi snatched the wood that Rann had dropped inside the door. The end was still smouldering. She leapt towards the wolf, spearing its flesh. It howled in agony, turning around. Its gnarling teeth dripping with Rann's blood. Delphi stepped back, holding the length of wood out, now covered in the wolf's own blood.

'Rann,' Delphi said nervously.

'It bit me,' he replied, his voice stammering, blood streaming from his wound.

'Can you move?'

The wolf eyed Delphi, and started to circle her, biding its time.

'Kill it!' Rann ordered, dragging his body to the side of the enclosure, and gripping the fence.

'Come towards me, Rann,' Delphi instructed, not taking her eyes off the wolf.

From behind them came a spark of fire. Suddenly the aviary and surrounding area was flickering in red and yellow dancing light.

'Get back,' Clem yelped, pushing her flaming spear towards the wolf, making it back up.

Delphi went to Rann and he wrapped his arm around her shoulders. She could feel his warm blood on her. They stumbled back and leant on the door frame.

'Clem!'

Clem thrashed her stick at the wolf as it easily moved out of striking distance.

'Go!' Clem yelled. 'Get the door ready!'

Delphi stepped with one leg in the cage doorway and one leg out. She grabbed Rann and tossed him out. He gripped his side, blood seeping through his hands. Clem threw the fiery stick towards the wolf and ran to the door. The wolf was quick. It was a grey blur within the dying light. As Clem reached for the door, her hands outstretched, the wolf gnarled its teeth around her foot. Clem pushed Delphi out the door and slammed it shut, with her still inside. Delphi frantically tried to open the door, but Clem's forcefulness had bent the latch.

'Leave it, Delph,' Clem said, her voice soft.

The wolf gnashed her foot. Splitting the bones with its teeth. It started to drag her backwards.

'Rann, help me,' Delphi said, looking over her shoulder. She could see he was passed out and white as a sheet.

Clem freed herself momentarily. She ran to the door and slipped her hand through the wire, gripping the sliding mechanism. As the wolf rushed forward and struck her again, she bent the lock downwards, so it couldn't be muscled open. Delphi tried to grab her through the wire, but it was no use as the holes could barely fit her fingers through. She then tried desperately to bend the lock back, but it was too twisted. Tears streamed out of her eyes.

'Clem!'

Clem was dragged into the darkness. The sound of screams and growling echoed around the metal walls. Delphi looked away. Tears ran down her cheeks. Her lips and teeth were chattering from the horror of what she had just seen. The feeling of losing another person sat like a heavy anchor in her heart. Through watery eyes, she could see Rann in front of her, his eyes were wide open.

'Rann!' she yelped, leaning down to him.

From the ground sprouted small micro-pipes. They hissed a familiar gas that Delphi had smelt before. She stood up, and looked around, tearing her shirt off and covering her nose. She stumbled backwards, her head spinning wildly. Her legs started to give way and buckle, but she managed to grip the side of the house. She looked up to see a door open by the chute. Several figures emerged, all wearing protective gear and large, hooded masks with breathing apparatuses. One of them looked at her, she could see its pale blue eyes through the screen and it looked shocked to see her still standing. Her surroundings spun quickly, and her vison went dark.

Chapter Nine: At the End

Delphi opened her eyes and she was staring at the ceiling. But it wasn't in her bedroom. She was outside still. She could see a blue sky, with white fluffy clouds. These ones looked real. Air caressed her face. It felt fantastic. Fresh and clean. It smelt almost sweet. She sat up, her brain thinking instantly that it was a dream, until she saw the metal walls encircling her. To her right, the aviary was gone. There was no wolf, and no Clem. The memory was fresh and so clear in her mind. The sadness was reawakened and she felt the horrible sting of loss. She slowly got to her feet, her head still feeling dizzy. The house was still there, but the walls had been pushed further back. The yard was bigger and there was a sense of openness. She wondered if this was the same house. Or if she had been moved.

'Rann?' she said, looking around to the ground where she had left him. She looked up to the house and ran towards the front door.

Inside the foyer, she halted. The staircase had moved to the left. It was larger and curved upward to the second level. She looked straight ahead and could see the same hallway heading to the same kitchen. But was it the same? Her hands went to her head and she held them there, as if cradling her own skull. It's all mind games, she thought. Whoever it is, they are just messing with me. From the top level she heard a groan, then movement.

'Rann?' she yelped and bolted up the stairs to his bedroom. Panic was clear in her voice. She prayed that she wouldn't be alone. From the corner of her eyes, she could see there were four doors now, instead of three.

Inside the room a young man sat on the bed. He had shoulder-length hair and a chiselled jawline. His facial hair looked several weeks old.

'Who are you?' he said, looking concerned.

'I'm Delphi,' she said, stepping out of the room and looking down the corridor.

'You must be another new person,' the man said, standing up.

'I was just about to say that to you, but I think you might be in… my house?'

A young girl appeared from one of the middle rooms. She had short-cropped hair that was dyed fairy-floss pink. She had tattoos down one arm. She looked at Delphi and smiled.

'I'm guessing this is a new house,' she said.

'A new house?' Delphi echoed.

'The staircase is on the other side,' she noted.

'I noticed that too. I'm Delphi.'

'I'm Elastase,' said the man from the bed. He got up and stepped into the hallway. He was tall and towered over Delphi. 'But I go by Eli.'

'I'm Tetra,' the girl said, giving a shy wave to the others.

A heavy plonk came from the far end room and they all turned to see an elderly man with a long white beard and short hair, nearly balding, emerge from the room. His arms were long and snaked with aged veins. His eyes looked curious and suspicious.

'Pleasantries, okay,' he said, looking over the ledge to the level below. 'I'm Phosgene. But if everyone is shortening their names, I'll go by Gene.'

'Did you know what is happening to us?' Eli asked.

'No, but I think it's some sort of game,' Delphi said, looking back to him.

'Of course it's a game,' Gene grumbled, looking at cuts on his hands. 'Silver balls and wolves? We're in someone's sick fantasy.'

'So, by the sounds of it, we all experienced the same thing?' Eli said.

'But I've never seen any of you before… maybe we won something?' Tetra added, feeling very confused.

'Won? We're back in here,' Gene grumbled.

'It might be the next level?' Delphi said, trying to put all the pieces together.

'If this is a different house, it must be different outside,' Tetra said. She crept down the stairs slowly, careful to look around every corner and room before walking into it. Delphi and Eli followed. Gene waited a moment, then trailed behind them.

Delphi waited for Gene. He paused by her and they made eye contact. She took his hand and examined it.

'You had a wolf as well?'

'It sounds like we all had the wolf. It was huge.'

'How did you fight it off? It looks like with your bare hands.'

The cut wasn't deep, not deep enough for stitches. They zigzagged across his flesh and were still red from bleeding.

'We lured it upstairs, into one of the rooms. Then I killed it. With these two hands,' Delphi looked up at him. 'Then I woke up here.'

'How many were there…at the end?'

'It would have been just me.'

Delphi considered this for a moment.

'Guys!' she heard Tetra shout. 'You may want to come look at this.'

Delphi rushed outside with Gene following closely behind her. Tetra and Eli were both looking at a street in front of them.

'What is going on?' Gene said, stepping around them.

Before them, was a street with several houses.

Chapter Ten: The Draw

It looked like a normal suburban street. It ran the length of the area they were in with houses on both sides and the one they had just come out of. Delphi counted two houses on one side and only one house on the other side. There was also a small cluster of trees that looked like a small forest at the end of the street, a few feet away from the road. Tetra went up to the nearest tree and ran her fingers over its bark. It was real. She could smell its earthy aroma. Leaves fell from above as a light gust of wind broke from over the wall.

'A street?' Eli said, his hair flowing out behind him.

'Something doesn't feel right,' Gene noted, keeping on the footpath.

The curb and grass all looked fake and brand new. The asphalt on the road looked recently done and the trees still had up-earthed soil along the base. Delphi tried to listen over the breeze for the sound of machinery, or people, but she couldn't hear anything. She also felt that something wasn't right. It was as if the whole place was holding its breath.

'What do they want us to do? Live in separate houses?'

Clank! Clank! Clank! Clank!

From each house, came the familiar sound.

'It's happening,' Tetra exclaimed.

Gene turned and ran back into the house. Tetra looked at Eli, then Delphi. 'We'll go in separate houses, maximise our chances of getting one!'

Eli turned around and ran towards the house nearest him. It was a low-level house with wide windows and a garden with metal roses. Delphi knew she wouldn't make it. The two houses at the rear were too far away to make it in time. She sprinted as fast as her legs could carry her. The whole time she thought of Rann and Nerium. But as with all her memories, they were starting to fade too.

As she approached the house, she could see it was three stories with a wrap-around balcony and a tall, brick-looking chimney. There was no door in the front frame, so she ran straight inside. Twin staircases, one on each side curved upwards to the second level. She could hear the clank and grind of gears and shifting pipes within the walls. I just need to find the drain room, she thought to herself. She ran to the nearest hallway and looked through two rooms, both were void of furnishings, with no holes or exposed exit pipes. She then found the kitchen and could hear the metal ball hit the second level and roll over her head above. She followed it but came to a dead end in the pantry. Suddenly, the rolling ball shift east, then dropped down and Delphi could hear the familiar rolling of the last slide as it was about to be shot out of the pipe. She ran out of the kitchen and into a small, hidden doorway. Inside was one pipe and two holes on the ground. In the blink of an eye the ball shot out like a rocket from a cannon. It skidded across the ground as Delphi dived, seemingly in slow motion. Her fingertips grazed the ball as it disappeared down the hole.

'Damn it,' she yelled in frustration.

She stood up and heard rumbling from above her. She thought it may have been another earthquake, but the house wasn't moving. She slowly made her way out of the hidden crook and back into the open foyer. From upstairs she heard a door slam. She wasn't sure whether to run upstairs or run out of the house in case something terrible started to occur. She had a foreboding memory of a house beginning to shake.

'Hello?' she asked, deciding to stay in the empty house. 'Anyone there?'

There was no answer but the deep rumbling coming from somewhere in the house's guts. It sounded like a motor trying to start. She slowly made her way up the stairs to the second level. There were four doorways, all without doors. It was the same as the last house, each room held a simple bed and nightstand fashioned out of metal. The bed was made with a thin mattress, an equally thin sheet and an uncomfortable looking pillow.

'It must have come from the third level.' she murmured to herself.

She took one step at a time, listening for any movement. The last thing she wanted was for another wolf or animal to be in the house. As she rounded the bend in the stairs, she noticed the staircase ended in a door. The door was made of wood and it looked odd amongst the glimmering metal. It had a dull-gold coloured doorknob that looked weathered and old. She reached out for it with trepidation and tried to turn it, but it was locked. From outside she could hear the voices of the others. She turned away from the door, though still curious to know what was behind it. She ran out of the house and could see Gene and Tetra congregating in the middle of the road. Eli was walking across his lawn with a big smile on his face, tossing a silver ball up into the air and catching it.

'You got one!' Delphi said.

Tetra reached into her pocket and pulled out another. 'Me too. Wasn't easy though, almost lost my hand down that hole.'

Gene didn't look happy. 'I couldn't find the room with the hole. It was long gone by the time I eventually found it.'

'Next time,' Eli said, trying to comfort him.

'So, now we just gotta find the chute,' Delphi said.

'Is that what your team called it?' Tetra asked while they began searching the surroundings.

'Yeah, what did you call it?'

'The Draw. But I think I like the chute better.'

'What did it give you?'

'Bread, water. Fire and wood and then weapons.'

'Weapons?' Delphi quizzed, running her hand along the eastern wall, looking for micro lines. 'We missed a ball.'

'It helped us kill the wolf.'

Delphi suddenly felt small fissures in the metal. 'Here,' she said. 'Feels like a door.'

Eli heard her and walked over. He used his height to run his fingers up and around the outline. It was rectangle and deeply hidden in the wall.

'I think you're right. It must be where they come out.'

'They?'

'You didn't see them?' Tetra said, her eyes showing deep fear.

'I saw something. People in suits. Like… protective suits.'

'Yeah,' Eli said. 'When one of us got really injured, they came and got him.'

'What happened?'

'He fell from the roof trying to pry the metal off to get the balls inside. When he fell, he must have fractured something.'

'Did they just come in and get him, while you were still awake?'

'They rushed in and sprayed us. It didn't take long for us to pass out. My memory of what they look like is foggy.'

'Hey,' Tetra suddenly said, turning around in a full circle. 'Has anyone seen Gene?'

Both Eli and Delphi turned around, expecting to spot him along the long wall, or amongst the trees, but he was nowhere to be seen. From the centre of the street came a screeching, howling rush of flapping wings and then a hollow scream coming from Gene.

Chapter Eleven: Adrenaline

Gene was laying on the ground when they reached him. He was unconscious and had blood trickling from his nose.

'Gene!' Tetra cried out, leaning down to him. 'Gene?' she repeated.

Eli took his shirt off and wrapped into a makeshift pillow. He lifted Gene's head and placed it underneath.

'We need water and bandages,' he reached into his pocket and pulled out the metal ball. He handed it to Delphi. 'I think I know what to do. I have to stay with him, check his pulse and breathing and try stop the bleeding, you two go find the draw.'

Delphi took the ball and ran. She started from the spot where she had found the door and ran left, making sure the wall was no further than a foot from her right arm. She could hear Tetra behind her.

'I'll start in the other direction!' she called out, but Delphi didn't respond. The adrenaline pumping through her veins made everything cloudy.

Delphi sped up as her legs started to ache and strain. She came across the very last house where she had gone in looking for the metal ball when it was released. From behind, it looked dark and deliberately shrouded from view. The light got caught in the trees and was blocked by the house, making the small yard behind it all shadow. It was hard to hear anything from where she was. Inside the wall to her right she heard a slight, quick noise that was quickly hushed. She stopped abruptly.

'Hello? Who's there?'

Something bashed against the wall, from the inside. Delphi

stepped back, terrified.

'You need to get out…' said a female voice. It was soft and full of fear, then suddenly it was muffled.

Delphi leapt towards the wall and placed her hands flat on it. She placed her ear against the wall and listened. There was nothing. Someone on the other side was trying to communicate. This just added to her thought that this was all a game of some sort.

'Delphi! Over here!' came Tetra's voice.

Momentarily lost in her thoughts, she quickly snapped back to her purpose and bolted out from behind the house and onto the street. It felt strange running up a brand-new street, with fresh air in her hair and her feet pounding on something other than metal.

'Tetra!' she called out, only seeing Eli and Gene on the ground.

'Over here!' she called, from behind one of the two-story houses.

When Delphi reached the back end of the house, Tetra was standing next to a hole she had found. It was slightly higher in the wall then the one from the previous house.

'Delphi, here! I found one.'

Delphi yanked the ball from her pocket and slammed it into the hole without hesitation. From inside the wall came clanking, and the sound of shuffling. A few seconds later the chute opened. Tetra stepped forward and stood on her tippy toes to see what was inside.

'No…' she said, more out of frustration. She reached inside and pulled out four cannisters of water and a flashlight. 'This isn't what we asked for!' she howled.

Delphi snatched up the water and ran towards Eli and Gene.

'What did you get?'

'Only water and a torch, no medical supplies.'

'I think it's okay,' Eli said. 'Something hit him hard in the face. His nose isn't broken.'

'Sure feels like it is,' grumbled Gene. They all looked down at him.

'What was it? What happened?'

'Bats.'

'Bats?'

'I saw something open in the road, just over there,' Gene pointed to a small, nearly invisible circle in the road. 'It was like another draw… it opened, so I went over to it, thinking they were giving us something. And hundreds of bats shot out of it, hitting me across the face. That's the last thing I remember.'

'We have to get him off the road and onto a bed,' Eli said calmly. He looked up to Delphi and Tetra, and there was concern in his eyes.

Together they lifted Gene and took him to the closest house, which was the single level house Eli had caught the silver ball in. Inside, it was nearly identical to the others. It had one bedroom, a bathroom, a kitchen, and the drain room. They laid Gene down on the mattress and Eli cleaned Gene's nose with his shirt. The once white fabric was now dotted with blood. They gave him water and waited until he fell asleep.

'I'll come back to check on him periodically.'

'Do you think you may have been a doctor?'

'I think a nurse maybe,' Eli said, wiping his hands on his pants.

'Look!' Tetra shouted as they left the house and walked across the front yard. The small forestry that separated the four houses from the fifth had movement at the very top of the trees.

'Something's up there.'

Eli hurried across the lawn to the nearest tree and tried to eye what it was, while still maintaining cover. Tetra followed. Delphi watched the trees with scrutiny until she had deciphered what she was looking at. She stepped gingerly across the cooling road. The sun was now setting, making the air crisp and dry.

'They're still here,' she said.

'What are?'

'The bats.'

Looking to the topmost tree branches, hundreds of bats hung upside down, pecking at one another and jostling for position on the branch. They flapped their long, leathery wings and screeched. Amongst them was a single white bat.

'Can you see that?' Delphi said, pointing at it.

'What does it have around its neck?' Tetra said, shielding her eyes from the light coming through the ceiling as she looked at the isolated albino bat.

'A key card.'

Chapter Twelve: What Was to Come

'They didn't fly out the top because they're nocturnal. They don't want to compete with other birds and things that fly,' Tetra said.

Delphi looked at her surprised. 'I'd ask how you know that, but I can take a wild guess.'

Tetra shrugged. 'Maybe I worked with bats, or in a zoo?'

'Sounds like it,' Eli replied, giving her a shy smile.

'So, what do we do now?' she said, turning to Delphi and Eli.

'The key must be our way out of here.'

'At night, they will start to fly out the top, so we don't have long.'

'We have this,' Tetra said, holding out her metal ball. 'It might provide us with something to use?'

Together they marched back to the second house on the street and around the rear where the chute was located. Tetra handed the ball to Eli, who could easily reach the hole. He plonked it in and took a short step back. The cogs inside turned and the draw shot open. He reached in without hesitation and yanked out a rolled-up length of rope. The draw shut quickly.

'How is that going to help?' Eli said, staring at it.

'We make a rope ladder and swing it up to the branches above.'

'Then what?'

'We'll make a netting of some sort and catch it.'

Eli looked doubtful. 'A netting from what?'

'A shirt.'

They moved away from the rear of the house and back to

the single-story dwelling. Eli checked on Gene who was awake and in some discomfort. Eli retrieved his shirt and tied a knot in the sleeves and met the others around the side of the house.

'We need something to hold the end open,' he said as Delphi was tying knots in the rope about a foot apart. From far above them, a bat dropped from its branch, screeched, and swooped down towards the road. Delphi dropped the rope and covered her head. Tetra leapt onto the grass and Eli shielded his face from the swoop attack. It appeared not to be heading for them but curved upwards and flew towards the open ceiling. The sun was setting and casting a burnt orange glow across the skyline. Another two bats followed.

'Quickly,' Tetra announced. 'They are starting to leave.'

They stood at the base of the tree that held the white bat. Delphi had mixed feelings as she saw how injured Rann got when he fell from the tree. But that was metal, and this was wood. She was careful to throw the rope away from the bats, so she didn't scare them. It looped around a branch on the first try.

'I'll go up,' Tetra announced.

Before Delphi could protest, Tetra had already climbed the rope and was standing on the first branch.

'I think you've done this before,' Eli said.

Eli's shirt was thrown up to her. She broke off a dead branch that had a wide fork in the middle of it. She attached the shirt and knotted the head-opening around a branch to stop anything coming out of it.

'It's two branches up, Tetra,' Eli said, moving around the tree. 'It's by itself. You are gonna have to climb up a bit.'

Delphi and Eli moved under her as she yanked the rope up and moved up the tree. She reached the branch and could see the bat hanging upside down.

'Careful,' Delphi whispered, not loud enough to disturb the bats.

Tetra could see its pink eyes and small, curled claws. Its wings looked nearly transparent. From above her, several more bats took to the sky, shaking leaves down on them. The albino bat jolted and moved along the branch, flapping its wings in displeasure. Tetra swung the make-shift net towards it, scooping it up. The bat launched into the air, covered in the shirt. Tetra nearly fell. She gripped the tree and it tore some skin off her hands. Below, Delphi gasped, watching Tetra finally regain her footing. The bat tried to fly off, but the net and branch it was attached to were too heavy. It fell to the ground several feet away. Eli rushed towards it, unphased by the creature. He gently peeled back the shirt and slipped the small card-sized piece of metal from around its neck.

'Stand back,' he instructed, noticing Delphi behind him.

The bat crawled out of the shirt and sprung into the air, taking off into the darkening sky above them. Along the street they were standing on, lights flickered to life. Luminescent white strips lined the road. Delphi examined the card. It was plain silver, but if caught on the correct angle, she could see thin lines running down it, like a barcode. They went back to the tree and helped Tetra down. She looked at her hands. Small scratches covered them. Her palms and fingers were red and raw.

'What do you think it's for?'

'There was a door behind the forest, maybe it opens it?'

A sudden, shaking boom filled the street and all three were startled from the rumble. Looking around with uneasiness, they waited to see what was to come.

'What was that?'

From each house came the familiar noise of chutes opening.

Chapter Thirteen: Let Me Out

They all spread out, running to each house. Delphi ran back to the three-story mansion at the end of the road. She hadn't seen the chute when she was back there before. It was still blanketed in darkness but she was able to see the draw open at the bottom of the rear wall where it met the ground. It was too dark to see what was inside. Nevertheless, she reached in and pulled out its contents.

Tetra ran to her house. She went around the back and there was no chute. She ran her fingers along the walls, trying to feel for indentations. It was completely flat with no divots.

'Where are you?' she whispered to herself.

She ran around the front of the house and could see Delphi walking towards her. She gave her a wave and ran inside. She checked the kitchen and dining room, as quickly as she could, knowing perfectly well the draw would close at any time. She ran upstairs then paused unexpectedly. From the corner of her eye she saw someone move from within her bedroom. She gasped, her mind racing uncontrollably. From what she was seeing, it appeared to be a person. They wore the same decontamination suit as the others. It peered at her from behind the wall and quickly disappeared.

'Hey, don't be afraid,' she said, being afraid herself, but still stepping slowly towards her room. 'Who are you?'

She entered her room to find the person completely covered in an impermeable body garment. The facemask reflected and distorted Tetra's own image. The person wore thick gloves and heavy, industrial boots.

'Stay away,' it said. 'Let me out.'

'You're free to go. I'm not stopping you,' Tetra said, taking several steps back.

Suddenly, Delphi entered the house.

'Tetra! What did your chute have?'

'Delph,' Tetra answered back. Her voice and tone indicated something was wrong.

Delphi started up the stairs, very slowly. 'Tetra, what's going on?'

The person in the suit shifted awkwardly, shivering as if they were freezing to death.

'Listen,' Tetra said with a calming voice. 'We're gonna go and you do what you need to do…okay? We're not going to hurt you.'

'Who are you talking to?' Delphi entered the room to see the masked intruder.

'Delphi, we are going,' she said, nodding.

Delphi took several steps back, out of the room and down the hallway, past the staircase. Tetra followed, walking backwards to make sure she didn't take her eyes off the person.

'Let me out,' the masked person said again.

Tetra stepped back until she felt Delphi's hand touch her shoulders. The staircase was now between them and the intruder.

'Tell us,' Delphi said, her voice gentle. 'What do you want us to do? How do we get out of here?'

The figure walked briskly to the staircase and ran down it towards the door. Delphi and Tetra ran to the staircase but halted just before the steps. The figure stopped by the front door and turned towards them.

'The flood is coming,' it said, then turned and ran.

Chapter Fourteen: Follow Me

Eli stood in front of the rectangular groove in the wall. He slid the card through the indentation. Nothing happened.

'Try it along the top,' Tetra said.

Eli lifted the card up to the top line and ran it all the way along. The door remained closed.

'Guys,' came a voice from behind them. They all jumped from fright and turned to see Gene standing in the dark, dragging something.

'Gene? What are you doing up?'

'I heard the draw open and got up to see what happened. I figured one of you put the ball in.'

Delphi approached him to see what he was holding. Gene held it out for her to see.

'What is it?'

'I reached into the draw and pulled out these,' it was several lengths of wood, over seven feet long.

'What did you get, Delphi?' Eli said, giving up on trying to swipe the metal card.

Delphi reached behind her back and pulled out a long-handled hunting knife.

'Whoa,' Tetra said, suddenly feeling very anxious. She took a step back. 'Why would they give us a knife?'

'Or wood, or a rope?' Eli added.

Delphi looked to her feet nervously, then back to Tetra. 'Tell them.'

Tetra felt her throat restrict. Eli and Gene looked towards her, curious.

'There was someone in my house.'

'What?'

'Who?'

'I went into my house and they were there. In my room. It looked like I surprised them, like they had been caught out.'

'What did they look like?'

Tetra looked to Delphi for reassurance. 'In a suit. Their face was covered.'

'It's not like them to be caught out like that. Something must have gone wrong.' Gene seemed lost in thought.

'It said something,' Tetra said, looking from Gene to Delphi.

'The flood is coming.'

Eli ran his long fingers through his hair. He looked extremely worried.

'A flood?'

No one said anything.

'That may explain what I just found this morning,' Gene finally said, breaking the silence.

'Found? What did you find?'

'Follow me.'

Gene set the lengths of wood down on the ground and headed out towards the small forest of trees that separated the houses from the mansion. Towards the rear of the small woodland the trees were closely planted together.

'Here,' he said, pointing up.

Delphi was slightly concerned that he was here when they all thought he was resting. Perhaps he was trying to find his own way out she thought. Eli looked up. It was dark. Delphi reached for the torch and turned it on. It shone a cone of light halfway up the wall. There was a door. With a key card lock.

'I'm guessing that's our way out.'

The doorway had a foot long ledge jutting out of it, but it was far too high up to grab or climb. Plus, there were no branches that hung near it.

'How did you find this?' Tetra asked, staring up at the door.

'I was coming to find you guys.'

'Maybe they gave us the wood to build a ladder?'

'I thought that too,' Gene responded. 'But there isn't

enough wood. We wouldn't even make it halfway to the door.'

'There's plenty of forest wood.'

'I say we all get some rest. In the morning we'll come back out and take another look at it. We'll figure out a plan.'

'Agreed,' Eli said.

Tetra went to Delphi, 'I don't feel comfortable sleeping in my house now. Can I stay with you?'

'Wait, aren't we all sleeping in the same house?' Eli protested.

'Best we split up,' Gene added. 'If the spheres drop again the more chance we'll have of getting one. The more we get, the better.'

Eli nodded. 'Yeah. Good idea.'

'Tetra is with me. We still have three houses covered,' Delphi's tone was final. She waited for someone to protest her decision, but nobody did.

Chapter Fifteen: The Ocean

'This door is closed?' Tetra said in surprise, standing in front of the closed door.

'When I missed the ball it must have closed.'

'So, where's the drain room?'

It suddenly dawned on Delphi. 'You know what, I hadn't seen it…I'm guessing that was it.'

'Should we tell the others?'

Delphi thought for a moment but relented to her tired limbs. 'I don't think it's important to tell them right now. We can tomorrow.'

'Can I sleep on the end of your bed? If you don't mind?'

'I don't mind,' Delphi said, looking out the door to the yard. 'I'm a little shaken myself.'

'Do you think it was…deliberate?'

Delphi turned to her. 'What?'

'The person in my room.'

'What do you mean?' Delphi said, sitting near her. She could see Tetra was much younger than herself, but her eyes and wisdom appeared far beyond her years.

'Like someone was deliberately staying back… in my house to tell us something.'

'They did say a flood was coming… and looking up at the open ceiling, if it does rain, there isn't a cover from what I can gather.'

'So, maybe that's how we are going to get out… or how this will end,' Tetra said, bringing her knees up to her chest and hugging them tightly against her body.

'I'm going to tell you something that I didn't tell the others, okay?' Delphi said, fearful that giving her the information may either raise more questions leading to frustration or give her false hope.

Tetra looked at her, concerned. 'Okay.'

'When I went behind this house to look in the chute, I heard something bang on the wall.'

'On the outside?'

'No,' Delphi said, keeping her voice quiet. 'From inside the wall. It said, you need to get out.'

'Do you think it's the same person that was in my room?'

'It's too hard to tell. Their voices did sound similar, but… I heard them both unexpectedly.'

They both drank water and made their way upstairs. The sheets on the bed weren't soft, or even the right size. They were far too small and were square. They felt almost plastic. Delphi went around to all the other rooms and collected the other sheets and they made pillows by folding them up. The main bedroom was bigger and they were both able to lie side by side with plenty of room.

'I have memories of something,' Tetra said, rolling over to face Delphi.

Delphi was staring up at the ceiling. 'Of what?'

'Water. The ocean.'

Delphi looked at her. 'I think I know what that is… but I can't really picture it. Not being there anyway… like I've seen it in a book, a long time ago.'

'I think I remember smelling it.'

'What did it smell like?'

'Salt.'

Delphi closed her eyes and reopened them. She wasn't sure if a second had passed, or hours. She turned to look at Tetra. She was facing the opposite direction, snoring softly. Delphi smiled and closed her eyes again.

Clank!

Delphi's eyes shot open. She instantly heard the click and rolling of a ball above her. It was moving quickly. Tetra had already leapt from her side of the bed and was heading for the stairs.

'Tetra! Wait!' she hollered after her.

Delphi followed her down the stairs, but she was too fast. Still feeling half asleep and slightly disoriented, Delphi momentarily lost Tetra in the maze of hallways and rooms.

'Tetra!' she yelled, seeing her shadow move in the dark.

Tetra ran straight into the drain room at the end of the hall. Delphi was running towards her as fast as she could, but she couldn't keep up. Tetra reached her hands out as the ball shot out of its spout and flew through the air. It slipped through her hands, her fingers sliding off the cold surface of the ball. It hit the ground and bounced.

'No!' Tetra cried out in frustration.

As it rolled towards the hole, Tetra started to scramble for it. Delphi reached the room just as the door began to close. Tetra had a look of absolute terror as the ball rolled its way down the hole. She fumbled her hand into the drain, trying to snatch it out. From behind her she could hear the door slam shut. Delphi had tried to hold it open, but there was too much force behind it. 'Tetra!' Delphi screamed, bashing on the door with her fists.

'Delph!' Tetra screamed from inside the drain room.

'Don't move! I'll go get help!'

Delphi ran back through the house and out the front door. She ran down the balcony stairs and suddenly felt a shock of cold around her feet and ankles. She looked down to see she was standing in several inches of cold water. Slowly, she looked up. The entire street was immersed in water.

Chapter Sixteen: Vault

Gene woke up to the sound of running water. He went outside to investigate. It was still dark. He could see water flowing from small grates that lined the street. Without caution or concern he wandered over to look at them. Kneeling down, he inspected the grated drain. It appeared clogged with darkened water. Dipping two fingers in it, he brought it up to his nose and smelt it. It did not smell drinkable. It smelt like copper. He stood up with his knees popping and back straining, but he ignored them. He thought of checking on everyone, but he thought better of it. They deserved to get as much sleep as they could. He went back inside, drunk from his canister and waited for daylight.

He grew increasingly tired and went back to bed. He lay awake for a few minutes thinking of the water and how long it would pour into the streets. At the rate it was flowing he expected it to take days, if not weeks for the entire area be swimming in a foot of water. Closing his eyes, he thought of the water and the drain holes in each house. Maybe they are linked somehow? He thought as he drifted off to sleep again.

His eyes shot open at the sound of clanking from above. He could see streams of light coming in through his open front door. He was about to run to the drain room when he noticed three balls sitting on his bedside table. He grabbed them and shoved them in his pockets as he rushed from the bedroom and into the drain room that was two doors down. As he entered, the spout spat out the sphere and he caught it mid-air.

'They are getting quicker,' he said to himself.

Reaching into his pocket, he pulled out the three spheres

he had snatched only a moment ago. One was red, one blue and one green. He held them up to the slither of light dancing across the walls of his house. They were not painted, the colour appeared to be integrated in the metal. A scream broke his concentration. It was coming from outside and down the street. He slammed the spheres back into his pocket and bolted outside. Splashes of water soaked his shoes and pants. He looked down, noticing the water had increased exponentially since he saw it a few hours ago. Delphi was sprinting towards him. Her face was stricken with terror and her eyes were wide.

'Tetra! She's locked in a room! Quick.'

'What? How?' Gene said, running towards her.

Delphi turned to head back into the mansion with Gene close behind her.

'The drain room was open. We woke when the sphere dropped and she ran straight in there.'

'Did you see it shut?'

'Yeah, it shut by itself.'

As they entered the house, Delphi was still in panic mode. Down the long corridor, Gene could see the closed door. The sun had illuminated the hallways and rooms, giving an eerie, streaky light.

'Tetra?' Gene said, his open palm on the door.

'I'm here,' she said through the metal door.

'Are you okay?'

'Yeah. It's dark in here.'

Delphi looked at Gene. She wanted to cry but pushed her emotions down. 'We'll find a way to get you out, okay?'

'What's going on?' Eli said, looking confused as he entered the hallway. 'I heard screaming, then I saw you guys running.'

'Tetra is locked in the room.'

Eli reached into his pocket and pulled out three balls. 'Maybe these have something to do with it?'

Gene turned to look at what he was holding. 'You got those too?'

'Where did you get those?' Delphi asked.

'They were just beside my bed,' Eli replied.

'Same.'

Delphi sprinted upstairs to the master bedroom. On her bedside table were the three balls. She grabbed them and went back downstairs.

'These were beside my bed. But there were none on Tetra's side.'

'Maybe there's only one set per house?' Eli said. 'I'll go check the other houses.'

Gene was running his fingers along the door, then up and down the wall.

'Here!' he suddenly yelped. 'Another hole.'

Delphi ran her fingers across the wall until she found it. It was hidden in the metal. Camouflaged by shadow.

'Guys,' came Tetra's voice. 'It's getting harder to breath in here.'

Gene looked at Delphi. Her face had dropped in anxious thought. Gene stepped back and held his hands open. The spheres rolled around in his palms.

'These must mean something?'

'What if we put the wrong one in?'

Eli rushed back into the house. 'There was more. They must be Tetra's,' he announced, sweat beading on his forehead.

'We found another entry hole. We think these new balls have something to do with it.'

Eli leant down and looked into the hole. It stared back at him.

'I'm feeling dizzy,' Tetra said from inside the vaulted room.

'Just try to relax,' Eli said, his voice soft and calming. 'Take some deep breaths.'

'We have to hurry,' Delphi said, trying to hide her panic from Tetra. She could feel her fear of losing another person well up again. 'Try one.'

'Which one?' Eli said, himself fighting panic.

'Green means go, right?' Gene added. 'Like, everything's okay. Green is ripe, or healthy.'

He plucked a green sphere from his pocket and slid it in the hole. It clunked and rattled, spinning down a long pipe. The sound of grinding gears and cogs echoed from under them. From behind them, they heard the outside chute open. They all looked at each other.

'Was that the...?' Gene said, confused.

'That doesn't make sense,' Eli said quizzically.

'I'm not going to find out what's in it, I'm staying right here, with Tetra,' Delphi stated. Images of Rann and Nerium floated in her mind. Their facial features were starting to crumble as the memory of them faded.

'I'll go,' Eli said eagerly and ran out of the hallway.

Gene looked at Delphi, 'We still have two more colours, and a plain metal ball.'

'Guys,' Tetra said. 'It's getting harder to breath in here.'

'Tetra,' Gene said, 'sit on the floor if you're not already and relax as much as possible.'

'We're working on it,' Delphi said, trying to give her encouragement to stay hopeful. 'What if this entry hole doesn't open the door? And we are just making things worse?' Delphi said, looking at Gene.

Gene looked to the door, as if trying to see through it. 'We can only try, right?'

'Yellow.'

Gene lifted the yellow sphere up to the mouth of the hole and paused just at its entry. He held his breath and let it go. The ball slid down eagerly. It rolled around in its tubing, clanking against metal flaps and doorways until they couldn't hear it anymore.

'Tetra?' Delphi asked. 'Did anything happen?'

'A light came on,' Tetra replied. Her voice was soft and staggered.

'And the air?'

'Still...hard to... breath.'

'Only red left, and the metal one.'

Delphi looked at Gene, waiting for him to come up with the answer. But they were both stumped for a decision.

'Do it,' Tetra said, from inside the room.

They could hear the desperation in her voice. Gene slid a red ball into the slot. He closed his eyes and listened to the mechanics under the house swallow it.

'Something is happening,' Tetra exclaimed.

'What is? What can you see?'

'The floor…it's separating… it's opening up.'

'Stay calm, Tetra. It's going to be okay.'

'It's not stopping!' she screamed. 'The floor is peeling back. There's nothing in here to hold onto!'

'Tetra!' Delphi screamed, bashing on the door incessantly.

They heard a heavy clunk, followed by Tetra's hollowed screams.

Chapter Seventeen: Of Us

'The key card!' Delphi suddenly remembered.

'I don't have it!' Gene shouted back, eyes frantic.

'Eli!' Delphi said, running out of the house.

Just as she rounded the corner, she saw Eli coming back from the chute. He was cradling something in his hands, tears streaming down his eyes.

'Delphi, I have to show you this.'

'We need the key card! The one from the bat!'

He dropped what he was holding, hearing panic and fear in Delphi's voice.

'Here,' he said, yanking the card from his pocket.

Delphi snatched it and ran back inside. Gene was trying to pry the door open with his fingers. His fingernails started to bleed.

'The card,' she said, with a hint of desperation in her voice.

Gene took it and slid it down the side of the door. It didn't budge. 'It must be here somewhere?'

'Maybe here,' Delphi said, frantically looking around the handle. 'Here!'

There was a thin indentation. Gene swiped it and the door popped open. Delphi pushed past him and ran inside. It was empty. The room was twice as big as her bedroom. Each side sloped down to a centre hole, no bigger than the palm of her hand. In each corner, where the wall met the ceiling, a spout extruded. Delphi dropped to her knees and thumped the ground with her fists.

'Damn it.'

'It's not your fault, Delphi,' Gene said, putting a calming hand on her shoulder. It didn't calm her, but still felt reassuring, like she wasn't alone.

'Why are they taking us?'

'It's a game we have to play. To the end.'

'But what's the end? When is the end?'

Eli was standing at the doorway, too afraid to go in. Gene sensed he was there and turned to look at him.

'What did you get, Eli?'

'You're not going to believe this.'

Delphi got up and wiped her tears away. 'What is it?'

'A photo album.'

Gene looked from Eli to Delphi, then back to him. 'A photo album? Of whom?'

'Of us.'

Outside, Eli went back to the place he had dropped it and picked it up. It had fallen into an inch of water and was dripping wet. He opened it up to the first page and there was a picture of himself, with a woman and a child.

'You and … who's the other person?'

Eli felt his throat clinch up. 'I don't know. Maybe my wife and kid?'

'Do you remember his name?'

'No,' Eli said, a tear slipping over his lower eyelid and rolling down his cheek.

The next page showed Delphi on horseback. She looked younger and was wearing an oversized cowboy hat. She was pointing into the sunset, with a huge grin on her face.

'Your horse?' Gene asked.

'I wish I knew,' Delphi responded, feeling crestfallen. It was a beautiful horse and Delphi felt a twang of kinship towards it.

Eli turned the page. The next photo showed Gene standing in military attire. He was next to a monument and looked several decades younger. With no beard and short hair, he was barely recognisable.

'Whoa, Gene!' Eli yelped, 'look at you!'

Gene was quiet for a moment. He studied the picture, taking in all the details.

'I don't recognise the insignia on my chest,' he finally said.

Delphi looked closer. She didn't recognise it either, or the place.

'Well, you were in some sort of military service.'

'I look no older than twenty,' he replied.

Delphi took her eyes from the photo album and looked towards the road. A soft wavering noise was gaining momentum several feet away. She peeled herself away from the group. Coming down the grass was a steady stream of water. It pooled around their feet. Gene and Eli hadn't noticed, as they were still looking at the book. Delphi walked up to the road and could see the bubbling holes along the asphalt were now fully covered in a foot of water.

'Guys,' she said. 'You better come up here and look at this.'

Gene folded the book shut and they both joined Delphi by the road.

'It's filling up.'

'It's the flood. It's coming.'

Gene turned over his shoulder and looked up at the doorway high in the wall.

'Maybe that's how we get out. We swim.'

'I can't swim,' Eli said, sheepishly, as he turned back to the group.

'I'm no Olympic champion either,' Delphi replied.

'Between the roof of the houses, the rope and the trees, we should be able to get across to the door.'

'What about these?' Delphi said, holding the coloured spheres in her hands. 'They might do something else.'

'We don't want to start opening hatches or doors when we don't know what is behind them,' Gene protested. 'If we open the wrong one, who knows what will happen.'

'So, you want to just stand here until the water fills up over the houses and swim to the door?'

Eli felt uncomfortable with the sudden tension that was building. He spoke up, 'I say we all return to our houses, look for other holes, or hidden doors… if we find anything… we yell out. If we don't… we all use the red ball.'

'Why the red?' Delphi said, her words spilling out of her mouth quicker than she could catch them. 'Red opened up the floor and it swallowed Tetra.'

'We use red first… because it's the worst,' Gene said gravely.

Eli nodded his agreement and both him and Gene looked to Delphi.

'Okay, but only after we search the houses.'

Chapter Eighteen: In a Line

Eli ran his fingers along every wall in his house. The only grooves he could find were where the wall met the ceiling, or the floor. He stood in the drain room and looked into each pipe but could only see darkness staring back at him.

'Hello!' he shouted into one of the exit holes.

He put his ear to it but couldn't hear his echo. Kneeling down to the ground, he pressed his face against the drain, to try see as far as he could. The hole was bigger than the pipes that the balls came out of, but not by very much. Cool air was wafting out of it. He guided the air with his hand, breathing it in. It smelt cleaner, and it was much, much cooler than the air outside. Slowly, he placed his hand over the hole, covering it completely. Before too long his hand became so cold he had to remove it. It was as if a refrigerator was below. Eli leant even closer, his eyes mere millimetres from the hole.

'Hello?' he said again.

He could hear cogs and machinery turning and grinding. Gingerly, he moved his fingers towards the hole, pausing momentarily right before his hand disappeared down it. Feeling around, he could only touch the surface of the walls. Without caution, he put his forearm down as far as it could go and felt around with his fingers. The cool breeze suddenly stopped. The teeth of the cogs moved slowly, then, without warning they whirled to life, cranking their teeth, and sending grounded flakes of metal up the tube. Eli yanked his hand out and checked his fingers, they were all there. From outside, he could hear someone yelling. It sounded like Gene. He ran to the door to see him across the road, standing on the porch of his house.

'Nothing in here!' he yelled.

'Nothing here either,' Eli yelled back.

Delphi emerged through the small cluster of trees, 'Nothing.'

'We'll all go to the holes and count loudly to three, then drop the red ball down,' Gene instructed.

Eli nodded and looked towards Delphi. She nodded and turned to head back to her house. She looked down and noticed the water was now up to the middle of her shins. It was filling up quicker than predicted. She rushed back, the water slopping up onto her pants and wetting her shirt and arms. She ran around the rear of the mansion and readied the red ball.

Gene hollered the first count, 'One!'

'Two… three!'

The red balls dropped down the metallic throat simultaneously, sliding and spinning until they reached something far below, bouncing along a conveyer belt. Delphi stepped back, waiting to hear what was to come. She looked at the chute, but it did not open. Suddenly, the trees around her started to vibrate. She ran to the front of the house and saw Gene and Eli running towards her.

'The trees!' Eli said, pointing to their peaks.

The very tops of the trees were shaking now. Leaves were falling all around them. The branches were thrashing wildly. Delphi ran to the road, almost slipping in the water. She looked up, just in time to see several large boxes fall from the cluster of branches. They fell several feet before snapping back and hanging, swaying from left to right. Red rope was tied around them. The rope went straight up to a hooked notch in the treetop. As soon as they had fallen, the trees had eerily stopped moving. Gene stepped towards them.

'What is it?' He craned his head back to look up at the boxes. They were about two feet long, and one foot high. Gene counted four boxes, all hanging from different trees.

'We'll never be able to reach them,' Eli said, approximating they were more than 14 feet in the air.

Eli waded through the water to one of the trees and placed his hand on the trunk. He thought about climbing it. He weighed up how far the trunk went until it reached branches where he could hold on without slipping back down.

'Look,' Delphi said. 'They seem to be in a line from your house, Eli.'

Eli stepped back to get a panoramic view of the trees that held the boxes. The four boxes wrapped in red rope started from a tree near his house, then ran in a straight line to the door in the wall.

'I'm guessing they each hold something to help us?' Delphi said.

'Or hinder us,' Gene replied.

'We still got plenty of spheres left, maybe we could–' Eli's sentence was cut short by the sound of clanging metal. He spun around to see something moving at the very rear of the roadway.

'What was that?'

'Look, a door is opening!'

Eli narrowed his eyes and could see, far in the rear of the massive arena, a large sliding door was opening. Delphi looked down and could see the water starting to flow towards the door. Gene started to run. He lifted his legs high. It was almost comical. He bolted for the door. Eli was close behind him.

'Hey!' Gene screamed, racing past the houses.

'Stop!' Eli echoed his pleas.

Delphi was behind them. Then she halted. From inside the doorway came several figures wearing black. They had large rubber gloves and covered their faces with masks and hoods. The rim of the face masks were bright yellow, as were the stripes around their gloves and boots. They were pushing something large.

Gene suddenly stopped, but Eli kept going.

'Eli,' Gene called for him. 'Wait!'

Eli sprinted as fast as he could towards the open door. Several figures emerged, pulling large ropes attached to something still hidden in shadow.

'Eli!' Delphi yelled.

One of the hooded figures pulled a small weapon from its belt, stepped forward and aimed it at him. Eli didn't stop. Water splashed up in large bursts as he got closer. The figure aimed and shot. Long, wire tendrils spat from the gun, spearing through the air, and attached themselves to Eli's chest. In an instant he was electrified. His body shook and thrashed until he fell into the water. Gene gasped and ran towards him but stopped when the figure moved the direction of the pistol towards him. From the cloudy shadow within the wall came a large, wooden boat. It was being dragged and pushed by several figures on what appeared to be a conveyer belt. Once it was free of the doorway they unlatched the ropes and sped back inside, the door closing behind him. Gene and Delphi ran to Eli. His head was underwater. They scoped him up and held him.

'Eli!'

Eli opened his eyes and coughed up water. He spat and tried to get to his feet.

'Wait, stop,' Gene ordered. Holding him down. 'They electrocuted you.'

Eli's eyes fully popped open as he stared at what they had released. A Viking longship bobbed up and down in the water in front of them.

Chapter Nineteen: The Teeth

Gene stood marvelling at the vessel. It was half the size of the ones he could vaguely see in his memory. It didn't have a mast, but there were two wooden paddles on each side. Delphi was helping Eli stand upright as he stretched his limbs and tried to shake off the buzzing feeling. His fingertips were numb and he had difficulty standing.

'That was dumb,' Eli told himself. 'All I was doing was trying to get through the door.'

'They didn't like you getting close to them,' Gene muttered, still looking at the boat.

'Yeah, well, if you had come closer, or even tried, maybe one of us could have gotten in the door.'

Gene turned to him. 'Then what, Eli?' he said, his voice raised. 'We can't fight off all six of them. There would have been more beyond the door.'

'We don't know that.'

'Do you think this is all run by six people in masks? I highly doubt it.'

'We could have tried, at least,' Eli said, turning away from them.

'Where are you going?' Delphi said, deliberately keeping out of their disagreement.

'I'm going to lie down. I have a headache and my chest hurts.'

Eli walked towards his house, sloshing through the water, and disappeared through the door.

'You shouldn't have been so hard on him, Gene.'

'Me? He's the one that put us all at risk.'

'I don't want to fire everyone up again, so we'll just drop

it.'

'Fine with me,' Gene said, running his hand along the wooden boat. He walked around to the bow. The wooden front had an elongated neck with a carved dragon head. Its popeyed features and gnarled teeth gave it a fierce, foreboding appearance... For Gene, it looked familiar, like he knew it. He knew it was based on something old. This wood, he thought, it isn't old. It's a replica. And much, much smaller.

Delphi looked from the boat to the doorway at the far end of the arena. It sat in the wall like a picture frame.

'The water fills up... we get on the boat, and head towards the door.'

'It can't be that easy,' Gene said, grasping hold of one of the oars and levering himself up onto the edge of the vessel. He slid down onto one of the seats. 'What about those boxes? Surely they mean something.'

'Maybe we need what's in them once we get to the door?'

Gene looked in the general direction of the boxes. 'You don't think that's the end?'

'I hope it is,' Delphi replied, sounding a little despondent. 'But if it's not, then we have to be prepared.' She hoped it wasn't another set of houses containing mysterious events.

Gene looked through the boat for anything hidden. There were no holes, or spouts for the balls. No hidden key slides or drawers on any of the surfaces.

'We wait for the water to rise. Paddle the boat to the boxes, retrieve them, then over to the doorway. I'd say with the rate the water is filling up. We could be okay tomorrow to start moving the boat toward the door.'

Delphi let the plan sink in. An ear-piercing scream ripped along the water's surface. It was a scream of horror and agony.

'Eli!' Delphi howled, knowing that wasn't a moan of someone awakening from a nightmare, but one of intense pain. She bolted for his house.

Water splashed up soaking her clothes as she entered Eli's house. She ran into his bedroom to find him clutching his leg.

'Eli? What is...' She took a step backwards. Eli's leg was

trapped inside a large metal cube. 'What– what happened?' Delphi said, kneeling down beside it.

'Delphi, help me get it off, it feels like a beartrap!' Eli was squinting his eyes and tears were streaming down his face.

Delphi ran her hands all over the square box. It was completely solid. Gene ran through the door, expecting to see Delphi consoling Eli. His mouth dropped open as he saw Eli's leg in the cube. He rushed to Delphi's side and produced the key card from his pocket.

'There's no slide to open it,' Delphi said with panic in her voice.

'It feels like it's eating into my skin!' Eli yelped. Both his hands gripping his shin.

Delphi suddenly shot up. 'Give me all the green balls,' she demanded, holding her hand out.

'Wait, what?' Gene said, slowly standing.

'Green's go, right? Green is everything is okay, you said it. They have to give us something to help him.'

Eli tried to lift his leg, but the cube was too heavy.

'Just wait a minute, before you rush off and do something stupid.'

'Stupid? It's gonna gnaw his leg off if we don't find a way to open it.'

Eli reached into his pocket and took out the green ball. He handed it to Delphi, 'Take it! Take mine!'

Delphi ran to the rear of the house, pulling her green ball out as she approached it. The water was now nearly up to her knees. She slammed one in after the other and waited. There was silence. She bashed on the chute with closed fists.

'Please!' she pleaded. Still the chute remained closed.

As she waded through the water, she could hear Eli inside, howling in pain. She rushed up the stairs and in through the long hallway. Gene was standing there with the green ball in his hand.

'I know what you're gonna ask me but hear me out.' Gene said, sliding the ball back in his pocket.

'We don't have time to argue, Gene. Give me the ball,'

Delphi demanded, holding her palm out.

From the rear room, Eli's agonising howls could be heard.

'What if I give you this and nothing happens?'

'Give it to me, Gene.'

'Listen, wait… what if we need it?'

'Gene… I'm not going to ask you again.'

Eli could feel the teeth clench hard from inside the cube. He lay back on the bed, his hands over his mouth trying to muffle his screams.

'I'm telling you, Delph, this may not work,' he finally held out the ball.

Delphi snatched it from his grasp and bolted back to the chute attached to the house. She jammed it in hard, listening for it to release the hatch. She could hear the spring mechanisms and cogs twisting and turning from inside the house. The hatch didn't open. Eli's screams were suddenly gone. Delphi stepped backwards as all around her, several small hatches within the walls surrounding the houses started to slide open. Gushing water began to flood in. By the time she got back to the front of the house, the water had started to creep inside.

'What happened?' she shouted as she rounded the hallway and burst into the room.

'The teeth, it let go,' Eli said, looking down at the cube. 'But my foot is still stuck.'

'It worked,' Gene stated, turning to Delphi.

'We have another problem,' Delphi said, as water started flowing into the room.

Chapter Twenty: Crystal Clear

Night had fallen and the air became freezing. Delphi swum up to her front steps and stood in the front room, the water up to her waist, shivering. Her limbs had become hard to move and numb from being in the water. She waded through the crystal clear water until she got to the staircase that led upstairs to her room. She was exhausted from having no food. Even though there was no breeze inside the house her skin started to goosebump and become icy to the touch. Gene had returned to his house and used his one and only silver ball. It appeared to have stopped all the valves from releasing water. He stated he was going to sleep for an hour or two, then get up and move the boat towards the forest.

As soon as Delphi laid her head down on her pillow, she fell asleep. Foggy outlines of people and the picture of her on her horse entered her mind. It all swirled in the darkness, images trying to connect to one another. A memory, faded and hazy, surfaced. She was at a farm and she was much, much younger. They were visiting someone that she guessed to be her grandfather. It was possible he owned the ranch. She tried to read the sign above the barn, but it was indecipherable. The clouds were lime green and stagnant. Something smelled like rotting eggs. Her grandfather brought out a horse by a lead rope and tied it around the post.

'They'll be here soon,' he said and gave her a smile. It warmed her heart.

She shot up in bed with a loud gasp. Her heart was thumping wildly. A memory had gotten through, and it was real. It felt real. She could hear the lapping of water, so she ran out of her room and peered over the ledge. The water was nearly up to the second level. It had gone from clear to a soft brown colour.

'Oh no!' She tried to call out to Gene, but her voice was trapped within the house.

Slowly, she made her way down the steps until she reached the water and took a deep breath, diving down to the front door. The water was murky and there were twigs and debris floating throughout the house. She got to the doorway, pushed off with her feet and swam to the other side. Her lungs started to tighten as she emerged on the other side. She could hear chaos all around her.

'Delphi,' She could hear Eli's voice shouting to her. 'Get out of the water!'

She bobbed up and down, looking around frantically. Eli was on his roof. His foot still in the metal box.

'Delph!' Gene wailed. 'Get out! Now! Sharks!'

Delph felt her blood run cold. She swam to the window around the other side of the house as Gene and Eli yelled over the thrashing of water gushing in through the open valves. She reached the windowsill and clawed her way out. As she hung on by her fingernails, a long, dark shadow passed under her. It did a quick circle and came back. It was large and cut through the water with ease. The creature circled again, as if monitoring its prey and waiting for an opportunity to strike.

'Don't fall!' Eli said, cupping his hands around his mouth. 'Get on the roof, quickly!'

Delphi scrambled, gripping the metal trusses sticking out from the crudely built structure and successfully got onto the roof. She lay on her back trying to get her heart to stop pounding. Her mind was going a thousand miles an hour, trying to process everything.

Sharks, she thought. There can't be sharks in here. She sat up and looked out towards the middle of where the street once was. Several fins cut along the surface of the water, heading in her direction. She was at one end of the lake now, and Eli and Gene were at the other.

'We've been calling out to you for hours!' Eli yelped.

'I must have been fast asleep. How did this happen?'

Gene was staring at the boat, while standing on his roof. The boat had floated towards the side wall when the water increased. It was gently knocking against the metal, making a clanging noise.

'The water flooded in. It started hours ago, but we couldn't get to you.'

'How did you get on the roof?' Delphi asked. 'With the box on your leg?'

'I woke up here,' Eli yelled back.

Why would they help us? Her mind was racing. Give us a boat, but fill this place with sharks? Gene walked to the edge of his roof. He looked like he was about to leap into the water.

'Don't do it, Gene!' Delphi screamed.

'I have to get the boat! It's the only way out of here. If the water comes up more, we'll all be washed away… and eaten.'

Delphi thought for a moment. 'I have an idea.'

Eli and Gene turned their attention to Delphi, who was standing with her toes over the edge of the roof.

'I'm going to jump into the water.'

'What? No!' Eli said, sliding his trapped leg closer to the ledge.

'It's the only way.'

'She's right,' Gene added.

'If I jump in, I'll attract their attention. Once they move here, Gene can get in the water and over to the boat.'

Eli looked to Gene for confirmation. Gene nodded diligently.

'What if… you can't get out in time?' Eli said, with worry in his voice.

'It won't happen, Eli. There are several trees close by. I'll just scramble up when they come this way,' she said, trying not to let the nervous thoughts exit through her voice. She knew her plan was good in theory, but the sharks moved with incredible speed. If she got stuck, she knew she wouldn't be able to outswim them.

She bent her knees and waited for Gene to give the signal.

He looked to the boat and saw a way to get up with ease. He waved his hand in the air and Delphi took a running leap into the air, landing in the water with a huge splash. Water filled her nostrils and she started to choke and flay.

'Delphi!'

She opened her eyes underwater and saw several dark shadows bolt towards her. She knew she wouldn't make it to the trees so she turned around and desperately started swimming back to the house. The shadows moved at an unbelievable pace. Delphi thrashed madly as she approached the house. She reached up with one hand and gripped the ledge. As her head rose out of the water, she could hear Eli yelling, but she couldn't make out what he was saying. She gripped the metal edge with her other hand, but slipped, falling back into the water. A large shadow was now directly under her. She tried not to look, but it was circling her. She swum a few feet to her right and tried again. This time, she successfully gripped the edge and managed to get her foot up and onto the exposed metal beam.

'Delphi! Hurry!' Eli howled.

As she lifted her other leg, a large shadow shot up from the depths of the water, knocking her with its snout. She rolled to her side, slipped, and started to fall towards the water again. Delphi tried to grip the roof, but her hands were wet, and the surface was too smooth.

'Gene!' Eli yelled, turning to watch him slide into the water and scurry towards the boat. 'Hurry, she's in the water still.'

Gene could barely swim. He flayed his arms about and kicked with his feet until he reached the vessel. He climbed up, slid over the side and fell flat on his back. He moaned and forced himself up. Using all his strength he pushed the boat off the wall and used the paddle to steer it forward. The boat curved to the right, heading away from Delphi.

'Gene! This way!'

'I can't do it by myself.'

Eli looked around to where Delphi was, but she had disappeared under the water.

Delphi swirled in a cycle of quickly moving water. She was upside down and sinking. A large shark circled her. Its menacing black eyes kept close watch on her, trying to figure out what to do with its find. Delphi lost all the air out from her mouth as she noticed another shark approach. Her lungs began to restrict. The second shark was much larger than the first, with an overbite showing triangular, serrated teeth. Delphi let her body sink to the ground and then she kicked off, darting in through the open door towards the staircase. The water was now over the second level. She was able to scramble up the stairs and stand with her head in an air pocket.

'Delphi!' she could hear muffled screams coming from the outside.

Panting for breath, she managed to yell back to them, but it didn't come out as a decipherable word, it sounded more like a painful moan.

One of the sharks entered the door. Its body barely fitting through. Its long head searched through the house for food. The second shark entered also, thrashing as its side fins rubbed against the door frame.

'What am I going to do?' Delphi gasped, realising the water was still rising.

Eli looked down at his foot entrapped in the metal box.

'Gene!' he yelled. Gene was getting closer, but still partially going in circles. He cursed and thrashed the paddles as hard as he could.

'When the sharks head towards me, I want you to shove the paddle down into the water so I can grab it… okay?'

Gene looked at him. Worry filled his face. He nodded. Eli held his captured leg over the water. It was heavy. He leant forward and stepped off the roof and into the water.

Chapter Twenty-One: A Frenzy

The sharks suddenly turned. Delphi watched them, trying to keep her head above water. They had come right up to the banister. She could see them in all their glory. Sandpaper grey skin and sharp, angular fins. The way they moved was effortless. But they had heard something and vanished quickly. Delphi swum towards the stairs and stuck her head in the water. She couldn't see them, so she swum down to the doorway. The water was murky but there was no movement. She went back up to the surface within the house and took a larger breath. This time she swum through the doorway and out, in front of the house. As her head breached the water, she could hear screaming and yelling. The boat was too far away for her to see. The only voice she could hear was Gene's. He was yelling and appeared to be crying. Delphi swum to the nearest tree and gripped it with all her might, pulling herself out of the water. She twisted her head around the trunk to see the boat was now at Eli's house, but he was no longer on the roof.

'Gene!' she called out. 'Where did Eli go?' As soon as the words left her mouth, she knew what he had done. Her heart had already been broken from the loss of Rann and Nerium, and now another blow. She wasn't sure how many more lost lives she could handle.

Gene was dangling over the side of the ship, his hand was gripping one of the long paddles, and he was spearing it into the water, trying desperately to get Eli to take a hold of it. Fins the size of coffee tables sliced through the water's surface, heading straight towards the boat. Delphi yelled out to Gene in panic. Why had he done it? To save my life? She pushed herself up the tree further, her legs wrapped around the thick trunk. The water around the boat suddenly went red. Gene stood up, tears pouring down his face and catching in his grey beard. He stared at the water as the sharks went into a frenzy. Delphi wanted to let go of the tree and fall into the water herself. Her heart sunk down into her stomach. Too many people have been lost, she thought. All energy and muscle strength went from her body. She was barely holding on. Whatever sick joke this is, it's over. They have won.

'Delphi,' Gene screamed out. 'Delph!'

Her eyes opened to see Gene paddling towards her. The boat was moving oddly, zigzagging with each heavy push of the oar. Gene would paddle one side, then leap over to the other side and paddle harder. Delphi was losing her grip slowly. She looked up at the tree to see if there were any branches to clasp onto and saw the hanging box with red rope tied around it. It was several feet from her head. She couldn't wipe the tears from her eyes, so she tried to ignore them the best she could. Raising one hand up the trunk, she slowly shimmied her way a few inches closer to the box. From the height she was at now, Delphi could see the dark shadows move through the water. The blood had dilated, and the thrashing of fins and teeth had stopped. She slowly etched her way up the tree. Her fingertips could just brush the bottom of the box.

'Delphi!' Gene yelled as the boat wobbled an indirect course towards her.

'Gene… I can get it…' she said, her voice strained.

'Forget it! I don't want you to fall in the water.'

Delphi ignored him and continued up the tree, her foot momentarily slipping, sending her down a few inches. Her legs gripped tighter and she hugged the trunk with her remaining strength. The large, blurry grey images of the sharks sped away from the bloodied water and back towards her. Gene was aiming the boat for the portside to slide right up against the tree. He was paddling and moving back and forth in manic, careless movements. Delphi reached for the box with one hand, it spun around, moving away from her. She looked at the boat as it came in under her and hit the tree. She pushed off it with her feet and gripped a top branch. Her body swung out from the tree.

'Delphi! Be careful!'

Delphi swung back, gripping her legs around the tree, and was able to undo the red rope. The box came undone, as if built to split open once the rope was loosened. Delphi lost her balance and fell from the tree. As she fell through the air, towards the boat, she looked up to see the box unfold and hundreds of silver balls explode from it. They rained down onto the boat as Gene tried to catch her. His arms were outstretched as she fell into them, but he didn't have the remaining strength to grasp her. She fell awkwardly on the bottom of the ship, with Gene falling to the side as the balls ricocheted off the wooden decking. Gene covered his face until they had stopped falling and rushed to Delphi.

'I'm so sorry, Delphi. Are you okay?'

'My back is sore, but I'm okay. I think my ankle is twisted,' she panted, trying to get as much oxygen into her lungs as she could muster.

Gene looked at her foot and could see the ankle swelling slightly. She moved it around in circles and winced. Something under the boat hit it hard, making the vessel shake from side to side.

'They really want to eat us,' Gene said half-jokingly, half panic-stricken.

'Let's get over to that door,' Delphi instructed, pulling herself up onto the side seat, next to one of the oars.

'What about these?' Gene said, holding up several of the silver balls that had dropped from the box.

'I'd say we are gonna need them. Once we get up there, we'll take as many as we can.'

Another hit came from under the boat, followed swiftly by another. Gene went to the opposite side and they started to row around the forest, now half submerged in water. As they approached the wall that held the door, they heard a noise from the other end of the now flooded street. The double doors in which their vessel had been released were now open. Portions of the wall on either side of the doorway had lifted up, like a drawbridge.

'Look!' Delphi said, pointing to the doorway. Inside was dark and flooded with water. There was no movement.

Gene looked at it with suspicion. 'I think it's either a trap, or they are coming for us.'

'Why would they come for us?' Delphi quizzed, confused. 'This is what they wanted, isn't it?'

'Maybe they didn't want us to get this far.'

The water was gushing in through the door, as if it were draining it away. Gene noticed it first as it was steering the boat off course. Several branches of the tree were now exposed out of the water.

'Hurry, Delphi! We need to get as close as we can!'

They began to row faster and faster. The vessel bounced off trees and skimmed over a house roof, grazing the bottom and scraping some of the wood off. The water had gone down a foot now. It was being syphoned faster and faster. They finally reached the wall and looked up towards the doorway. It was still several feet above them.

'Even with the rope, we can't latch it onto anything… it's no use,' Gene said deflated.

'What about tying it around an oar? Maybe we could stick it in the door frame?'

'It might work… but we are running out of time fast.'

Delphi looked down at the silver spheres. 'What if only one of us is meant to make it?' She looked up at Gene with wide eyes.

Gene looked at the silver ball in her hand. 'One of us? We won't let that happen Delphi. We'll both make it.'

'When we used a silver ball before, when Tetra was locked in the drain room, the water came in… it caused the flood.'

The boat rocked back and forth, gently tapping against the metal wall.

'One of us has to swim down there, put the ball in the hole

to raise the water.' Delphi nodded her agreement. 'We stand no chance against the sharks and whatever else has come in here since the flood door opened…. Whoever goes won't make it back.'

Delphi started collecting the balls from the bottom of the boat. She slid them into her pockets until they were bulging and heavy.

'It's got to be me,' Gene said. 'I can't let you do it.' His eyes started to gleam with tears.

'No,' Delphi said. 'I've lost too many people already. I'm not losing anymore.'

She stood on the edge of the boat as Gene lunged towards her to stop her. She dove into the water and let the silver spheres weigh her down to the bottom.

Chapter Twenty-Two: A Few Inches More

Delphi held her breath as her feet hit the bottom. She could feel the grass caressing her feet. Opening her eyes, she could only see a few feet in front of her. The colour of the water made it nearly impossible to see. She turned around, her cheeks full of air and headed towards the house. She knew she would run out of breath soon because her lungs were already sore from falling onto the boat. She moved quickly. She kicked off from the trees and swam as hard as she could. When the weight of the silver spheres were too much, she let some out of her pocket.

As she approached the house, she could feel her lungs tighten. The pain was intense so she released air from her mouth and nostrils. The air bubbles looked like open umbrellas as they floated towards the surface. She swum through the doorway and into the nearest room to find an air pocket to refill her lungs. The closest room was the dining room. She kicked and swam towards it. Suddenly, something grabbed a hold of her leg. She spun around to see one of the masked figures wearing a diving mask holding onto her foot. She screamed, letting out all the air she had spare. The diver yanked her leg, pulling her away from the room. Through the murk, Delphi could see there was another diver behind her. She kicked at the figure but missed. It grabbed her and pulled her out the door of the mansion. She steadied herself and aimed for its mask. She brought her knee up high and swiftly booted its mask off. It twisted to the side, broken, the glass visor shattered. Nerium's face stared back at her. Delphi's eyes peeled open in shock. Nerium was alive. It seemed like a lifetime ago. Nerium's eyes were completely white as she struggled to reattach her mask, letting go of Delphi's feet. Delphi felt her throat start to restrict and her brain cry desperately for air. She grabbed the banister to the staircase and pushed herself towards the room. She rocketed up towards the ceiling and split the surface with a huge gasp. There was only two inches of air between the water and ceiling. She tilted her head back, sucking in as much air as possible.

'Nerium!' she called out, her own voice echoing around the claustrophobic space. 'She's alive.'

Delphi knew she didn't have long. There was another diver behind Nerium who would be coming in the door any moment. She took another deep breath, emptied out several more silver balls and dove into the gloomy, brown water. She swum down the hallway, peering over her shoulder to see if anyone was chasing her. It was too dark to see. She reached the end of the corridor and took the remaining two silver balls from her pocket and pushed them into the hole. They were heavy enough to sink down into the mechanism. As she turned to head out of the corridor and back into the dining room, she came face to face with another figure wearing a diving mask. There was a tank attached to their back and a flow of bubbles pouring from their mouth apparatus. From below came loud clanking and gurgling. The figure held its hand out for Delphi to take. She was apprehensive, but fast running out of air. She took it and the figure turned using its flippers and dragged her out of the house. The water was completely cloudy now. Her vison showed less than one foot in front of her. As the figure took her up to the surface, Delphi noticed it was now higher. The balls must have triggered the flood again.

They broke the surface of the water. Delphi took a deep breath and could hear Gene yelling to her. Delphi looked around for the diver, but they were already swimming away, deeper into the darkened water.

'Delph! Hurry!'

Gene was waving the oar around in wild circles, trying to

get her attention. Delphi didn't think for a second. She kicked hard towards the boat. With every stroke of her arms, she filled her lungs with a desperate gulp of air. From the corner of her eye, she noticed how high the water had become. As she approached the boat, she glanced up at Gene. He had a look of absolute terror on his face. He was looking slightly behind her. Too scared to look around, she clutched the oar and Gene launched her out of the water. She gripped the side of the boat and flung herself in just as the massive jaws of a shark sunk into the wooden side. The sound of crunching timber turning to matchsticks made her stomach cramp.

'That was too close…whatever you did, it worked. The water is going up.'

Delphi looked down at her feet as she caught her breath, the boat was filling with water.

'How close are we?' Delphi said, her back still aching. She stood up and could see the doorway. It was only a few feet above her head. It looked like a metal door and handle that had sunk into the wall.

'Delphi, look,' Gene said, still holding the oar in his hand like a baseball bat. The water was slowly going back down. 'This can't be. They'll never let us win…or survive.'

Delphi looked out at the treetops before her. Before her very eyes, she could see the water receding.

Delphi felt her shoulders shrink down in into her chest. She felt utterly defeated.

'It was too risky going down there, plus,' she emptied her pockets, 'there are no silver balls left.'

The ones at the bottom of the boat had been washed out through the massive teeth holes.

'Get on my shoulders,' Gene said, dropping the oar.

Delphi spun around as Gene positioned himself against the wall.

'But what about you?'

'Climb up quickly, we don't have time to argue. You can pull me up.'

Delphi reached for Gene's shoulders and hauled herself up

his back. She placed her foot on his lower back, then his shoulders and pushed herself up the wall. Her fingertips caressed the ledge.

'A few inches more….'

Gene gritted his teeth and stood on his tippy toes. He moaned in agony, feeling the ship under him sinking by the second. Delphi slid one finger, then two, then her whole hand over the ledge and held on as Gene's shoulders disappeared from under her feet. She gripped the edge with her other hand and crawled with her feet against the wall until she could slide her elbow over the ledge. One leg swung up. She looked down and could see Gene staring up at her smiling. He was too far down now.

'Hold the oar, I'll pull you up. We can do this!'

Gene continued smiling. 'You know Delphi,' he said as shark fins circled the vessel. 'I think I'm okay with this. You guys have taught me a lot.'

'Gene don't do this. Hand me the oar,' Delphi's tears streamed down her face.

The vessel filled with water and Gene started hitting the sharks with his oar. Finally, the water engulfed the boat. He was still fighting when they took him. Delphi closed her eyes and sobbed loudly, rolling over onto the ledge.

She stayed laying there for several minutes, hearing the water get syphoned out until there was only sopping wet grass left. There was no evidence of sharks or anyone else. Even if someone had come to take her, she would have let them. She had barely any fight left. The vessel remained under her, now tens of feet below, chewed in half by ravenous sharks. She slowly got to her feet, feeling a bit lightheaded from being up so high. She turned the handle and the door opened. Looking inside, there were no discernible features. It was completely dark. She walked through into the darkness.

Epilogue

Delphi woke up in a room that she didn't recognise. It wasn't one of the rooms from the houses she had been in. It was painted burgundy red with a white tiled floor. The paint had started to peel off. She could see patches of white putty dotted around the ceiling. There was a large window frame on the left wall, but the glass was completely black. She was sitting on a cold, metal chair. In front of her was a metal table with a single glass of water on it. She reached for it and smelt it. It smelt clean and fresh, so she drank it feverishly. The door in front of her opened and a man walked in with short, neatly cut hair. The sides were razored to the skin. His complexion was nearly olive and he walked like he was in a hurry. He had long fingers and wore wire framed glasses. He had a notebook tucked into his armpit. When he reached Delphi he plucked it out and flipped through the pages. He looked up at Delphi and gave her a passing smile, before licking his finger and flipping through several more pages.

'We are calling you… Delphi? Is that correct?' the man said.

'I know that's not my real name,' Delphi said, with a belittling tone to her voice.

'No,' he said back, going back to the first page. 'It's not.'

'Tell me what it is.'

He looked up at her over the rim of his glasses. 'We can't tell you that… yet. What I can tell you is that Delphinium is a code name for you. The code names in the first trial are flowers, which I believe you figured out quite early on. Very impressive. We have not heard of anyone figuring that out before.'

'Who's we?'

The man looked over his shoulder at the door. 'If I told you, I would be in there with you.'

'You are in here with me.'

'No…out there,' he nodded towards the window.

'You know you're making me do this against my will? I'm not going back out there…. Let me go. I made it through whatever sick game this is. Now free me!'

'Game?' the man said, feigning laughter. 'This isn't a game. It's for the betterment of civilization. You are helping everyone by doing this. And it was your will to participate… you just can't remember it.'

'Why would I volunteer for this? To almost get killed?'

The man huffed and stared at her for a long time.

'You got the photo album,' he said, questioning himself. He flipped through the pages and ran his finger down a long list of items. 'Yes, says here you did.'

'We got the album,' Delphi said through gritted teeth.

'Did it trigger anything in you?' the man said, his eyebrows raising in curiosity.

'No… I have no memory of any of the pictures. No one did.'

The man laughed louder. This time it was real. 'Haha, no you wouldn't have. If you did, I would not be particularly good at my job now, would I?'

Delphi looked away from him. She couldn't stand his mockery. She tried to stand up, but her limbs felt too heavy to lift. She wanted to pick the chair up and throw it at him.

'So, it's your job to erase our memories? You seem pretty happy with yourself being able to harm others.'

'We didn't harm anyone. I assure you. When this is all over, we will show you.'

'What about Nerium?'

The man went back to his folder. He found Nerium's participation sheet. 'What about her?'

'I saw her in one of the suits.'

'Yes,' the man said, pushing his glasses further up the

bridge of his nose. 'That should not have happened. I must say, you are the first to see the reintegrating of the participants.'

'Participants? Is that what we are to you? Something to just use and toss away as you please?'

'Because you won't remember this, I'll tell you,' he pulled his pant leg up and knelt down in front of her. 'You go in, you play our "game" and you come back out and help. That's generally how it goes. However, the medicine we give you wipes all memory of you ever being in there.'

'She had white eyes.'

'A simple side effect of the memory drugs. But, before we go onto phase two, I wanted to show you this,' he looked towards the blackened window and nodded. The dark tint started to slowly lighten up. After ten seconds, it was completely see-through. Delphi managed to get to her feet. She half considered rushing him and bolting for the door, but she was too weak. She shuffled over to the window. She was looking down at the small street. It was covered in people pulling out the trees and putting them on the back of large trucks. The grass was ruined and the boat still lay in half at the bottom of the wall. A siren howled from somewhere behind her and all the people got in the trucks and drove out through the double doors. It shut behind them. Delphi looked over her shoulder at the man. He was smiling and pointed back out the window. She turned back to see it suddenly engulf in fire. It roared in a great fireball, tearing through the houses and turning the boat to ash. Delphi covered her eyes from the bright, burning light. The fire dissipated, leaving everything smouldering. She turned back to the man who had tucked the folder back under his arm.

'Everything has been wiped clean. No evidence you were there at all.'

'What now?' she snarled, sitting back on the chair.

'Now you go back in. We start again.' He reached into his pocket and brought out a black ball. He placed it on the table and rolled it over to her. Delphi snatched it up quickly. 'I'm not meant to give you that… but I like you. I've been watching you on the monitors. Don't tell anyone I gave it to you.'

'If I start again… I'll know everything in there… I'll know what to do.'

The man spun on his heels and headed for the door. He opened it and looked back at her. 'No, you won't,' he said and left the room. The door clicked shut behind him.

Delphi slipped the ball into her pocket just as the room was engulfed in a thick, mint green gas. Her vision began to spin and her head lulled forward. Her eyes closed. She tried to remember her horse as she fell unconscious.

Acknowledgments

I would like to thank Sabrina and Ouroborus books. Jenny for reading it and giving me notes on editing.

I'd also like to thank friends and family who support me.

The author would like to thank the University of Southern Queensland's Editing & Publishing students of 2021 for their assistance in this project, in particular Abby Rose, Anya Jarosz, Cassie Evans, Madeleine Warburton, Nicky Parigi, Sabrina Healy and Shelby Matheson.

For more information visit
www.ouroborusbooks.com